CLAIMED BY THE SHEIKH

DESERT KINGS, BOOK 5

DIANA FRASER

BAY BOOKS

Claimed by the Sheikh
by Diana Fraser

© 2015 Diana Fraser
Print Edition
ISBN 978-1927323175

With an arranged, love-free marriage looming, Prince Sahmir of Ma'in is enjoying his last night in Paris when Aurora runs by, fleeing for her life. All Rory wants is to regain the estates her father lost to the Russian mafia. She hadn't planned on marrying the Russian, or living with a sheikh and she certainly hadn't planned on a baby.

—Desert Kings—
Wanted: A Wife for the Sheikh
The Sheikh's Bargain Bride
The Sheikh's Lost Lover
Awakened by the Sheikh
Claimed by the Sheikh
Wanted: A Baby by the Sheikh

Print Edition

For more information about this author, visit:
http://www.dianafraser.net

This is a work of fiction. Names, characters, places, and incidents are the product of the author's imagination, and are used fictitiously. Any resemblance to actual events, locales or persons, living or dead, is co-incidental. All rights reserved. Except as permitted under the US Copyright Act of 1976, no part of this publication may be reproduced, distributed or transmitted in any form or by any means, or stored in a database or retrieval system, without prior permission of the author.

❧ Created with Vellum

CONTENTS

Chapter 1	1
Chapter 2	17
Chapter 3	35
Chapter 4	52
Chapter 5	69
Chapter 6	79
Chapter 7	97
Chapter 8	116
Chapter 9	131
Chapter 10	153
Chapter 11	175
Epilogue	192
Afterword	195
Wanted: A Baby by the Sheikh	197
Also by Diana Fraser	199

CHAPTER 1

*I*t was past midnight and the only sounds in the Place des Vosges were the lonely notes of Debussy that drifted through the open door, down to the steps where Prince Sahmir ibn Saleh al-Fulan stood drinking red wine and watching the snow fall.

He couldn't remember the last time he'd stopped to watch snow fall. Klosters maybe? Pre-teen definitely. Like intricate pieces of frozen coral, the snowflakes drifted down from the night sky in a lazy path, past the grey slate roof, and brick and stone striped façade of his Paris home, before coming to rest on the glossy pavement. As insubstantial as they were, they were beginning to accumulate, lightening the square to a world of white.

Sahmir narrowed his eyes against the glare. He'd spent too much time in heavily curtained hotel rooms—gambling by night and trying to forget his past in the arms of women by day. Too much darkness, too little light.

He let one flake settle on his hand and remembered how snow had fascinated him as a boy when he and his mother had left the heat of Ma'in for their annual holiday in Switzerland. He felt a flicker of that memory now, as he examined the white snowflake, momentarily perfect against his dark skin. He'd used to believe in magic, in fairytales. Where had that innocence gone?

The flake melted. He sighed, took another sip of red wine and looked across at the park where the snow was beginning to create shapes in the dark trees. He wouldn't be seeing snow again for a while. He'd done what he came to Paris to do. Now it was time to return to Ma'in, back to the responsibility he'd promised his dead sister he'd embrace.

Suddenly the sharp, urgent sound of stiletto heels unevenly stabbing the pavement came to him through the muffled, still air. He looked round to see a woman running along the street towards him. From the light of a street lamp he could see that she was tall and slender with long, dark hair that streamed behind her and she was wearing a bright red ball gown with a black bodice. No coat, despite the weather.

He could tell from the way she kept darting looks behind her that she was running from something or someone. And whoever that was had obviously put the fear of God—or the Devil—into her.

Don't get involved, the quiet voice of his sister whispered in his head.

He frowned, warring with the gentle voice that was the only thing which lay between him and trouble.

Don't get involved, it repeated. *Look what happened last time.*

As she drew level with him she turned to look behind her again and it was then that he knew he couldn't *not* get involved. Her eyes were wide with fear, but it was the vulnerability he saw there that shot straight to the core of him.

He barely felt his half-empty glass slip from his fingers as he pushed himself away from the wall and leaped down the steps and into the square after her. Whoever she was, wherever she'd come from, she needed help.

Aurora, Comtesse de Chambéry didn't bother to look which way she ran. All that mattered was that she got away from the man who she'd hoped would be her salvation, but who'd proved to be the total opposite.

Oblivious to the stares of strangers, not feeling the icy cold on her bare arms, she tried to outrun the memory of his eyes—cold and cruel—as he described in disgusting detail what he planned to do to her. Not only didn't she have a hope in hell of regaining her beloved estate, but he also didn't plan to release her until he'd got what he wanted from her. She could still feel the pressure marks on her arm where his fingers had gripped her, forcing her to hear him out.

She checked behind her. She couldn't see anyone. Not yet. But it was only a matter of time before her absence would be noticed and he'd send his men to follow her.

She ran on, but her bare shoulders were starting to ache in the icy air and her wet shoes cut into frozen feet that stumbled. Where could she go? She knew nobody in Paris.

She stopped running, suddenly aware that the street had given way to a garden, dense with the stark tracery of clipped limes topped with snow. Her hand instinctively sought out the wrought-iron gate as she looked up into the dark-limbed trees, remembering with vivid clarity her estate that was no longer hers.

There was a shout from behind her and with a panicked sob she fumbled with the iron latch and ran into the garden. She ran up the path towards the central stand of limes until she found her way blocked by a frozen fountain, whose smooth rivulets of water ran solid from its center, down into an icy, ruffled surface.

Heart pumping, she clutched the sides of the fountain and looked down into its opaque depths as she tried to regain her breath which heaved mistily into the freezing air, aware that the pounding of feet had also stopped behind her. There was nowhere else she could run. She would have to face the man who claimed he owned her family's estate and take whatever he wanted to do to her. There was no escape this time.

She took a deep, shuddering breath, willing herself to be calm. But when a large, male hand reached out and touched her arm she screamed, jumped around, twisted her ankle, and fell heavily to the icy ground. As she fell she saw the man's face—not the Russian's—and dark eyes, so concerned, so kind—so definitely *not* the Russian's.

"Mademoiselle, s'il vous plaît! Qu'est-ce qu'il y a?"

He leaned towards her—pressing down his arm to flatten out the skirts that billowed around her—and reached out for her hand to help her up.

But she didn't move. Whether it was the fear that her ankle wouldn't take her weight, or the relief that this man wasn't the Russian, she didn't know. It couldn't have been anything to do with the hand reaching out, but not taking, or those eyes, full of warmth and concern.

"Qu'est-ce qu'il y a?" he repeated.

"The matter?" She looked over his shoulder, then panicked as she remembered what exactly the matter was. "Everything." She accepted his hand and grimaced at the twinge in her ankle as he pulled her up. "I need help."

The smile vanished. "Tell me."

It was a command from someone used to giving orders. But it was a command she wanted to obey. "A man." She couldn't bring herself to say his name. She shivered and looked out of the square toward the road. It was empty. She felt his grip tighten on her hand.

"A man is chasing you?" The look of shocked outrage

confirmed her initial feeling that she could trust this stranger.

"*Oui.* I need to get away from him."

He frowned. "You must come home with me and I'll call a taxi to take you wherever you wish to go."

"No!" The idea of being trapped in a stranger's house, so close to the Russian's, panicked her. "No," she said more firmly. "I need to leave, to…." She trailed off, not knowing where she needed to go. Another shiver wracked her body, followed by another and she stumbled a little, her strength leaching out of her with the cold.

"Would you like me to take you to the police station for help?"

She shook her head. "*Non!*" The memory of the Chief of Police enjoying her captor's hospitality was proof the police wouldn't help her.

"Look, until you decide where to go, come inside my house for a few moments to recover. You won't go far on that ankle and you'll freeze if we stay here a moment longer. What you need is a stiff brandy and warm clothing, before you do anything. These things, I can give you." He took off his dinner jacket and swept it around her shoulders. "We're wasting time. If there *is* someone after you, then you'll be safer off the streets."

"But…"

He brushed snow from her hair. "Do you have a better plan?"

Plan? She'd only ever had one plan—to stay on the family estate which her father had ending up losing in a card game. "*Non*. No plans."

She tried to take a step forward but, whether from the numbing cold or a sprain, her leg gave way beneath her, and she stumbled. But, before she could fall, he scooped her up and brought her tight against his chest and began to walk back to the street.

"*Non!*" Her cry was instinctive and yet, strangely, she felt no fear. Only warmth as the heat from his body slowly calmed the shivers that wracked hers.

"Don't worry," his deep voice rumbled in her ear, pressed close to his chest. "I won't hurt you."

"No! I have to, to…"

"To what?" His voice was deep and comforting.

"To run away." She tried to look over his shoulder, but his arms held her too securely. All she could do was look up into eyes that held the kind of smile from which you couldn't turn away, the kind of smile that made you melt a little inside. It may have been calculated to charm, Aurora wouldn't have known with her inexperience—all she knew was that it was working.

"I think you've done that already."

"But where have I run to?"

"To me." He opened the park gate and they were once more on the quiet street. Perhaps he felt her tense at his words, perhaps he just wanted to hold her more firmly—whatever the reason, he gripped her body more tightly. "*Temporarily*, to me. Don't worry. I'll take you to my house and we'll work out how to further your plan of running away, then. When you're warm and safe."

"Safe…" She hadn't felt safe for a long time. She shouldn't feel safe now, in a stranger's arms, but somehow, she did.

She looked around the street, praying there would be no sign of the Russian. But there was no-one to disturb the snow that lay like icing on the road, on the old-fashioned streetlights, and on the pillars that held aloft the vaulted arcade which fronted the mansions. It was like a scene from a Victorian picture book, except for the fear that from behind each snow-topped bough, each corner of the square, the Russian would suddenly appear—large and angry.

Mercifully, the stranger must have understood something of her panic and he ran up the wide, deep steps of one of the houses to an open door from which light spilled.

She glanced down and noticed drops of red stuff on the snow. She stiffened and then saw that it was wine, only red wine. An empty glass lay next to it. But still she shivered.

Once in the hall, he closed the door with his foot and for one long moment they looked at each other under the bright hall light.

An undone bow tie dangled from his open shirt, and stubble on his chin darkened his already dark skin. She felt compelled to look higher on his face and wished she hadn't when dark eyes looked down on her from above high cheekbones. He was the most handsome man she'd ever seen.

She shifted in his arms. "Thank you, I…"

"Of course." He released her and she stood up, shivering almost uncontrollably now.

He brought her close to his side, supporting her and warming her at the same time, as they walked across the hallway to an open door from which music drifted. He was so close she couldn't help inhaling his scent—a blend of red wine, cinnamon and the watery smell of snowy fresh air. He smelled of Christmas. She closed her eyes more tightly and tried to stop a bubble of hysteria rising from deep inside. She didn't know whether to cry or laugh.

They entered the front reception room where a chaise longue was pulled up in front of a fire, burning low in the grate. All around, the furniture was covered in white dust sheets, like snow drifts. Gratefully she sank down onto the chaise.

"Don't move. I'll get a warm cover and a hot drink."

Move? She wasn't going anywhere immediately. Not just

because she felt safer with this man than running through the empty streets of Paris, but also because she sincerely doubted that her legs, numbed by the cold, would hold her. Shivers continued to wrack her body and she stretched out her hands—which looked as deathly white as the snow—towards the glowing embers of the fire.

Moments later he returned with a feather duvet which he tossed over her. She immediately felt welcome heat return to her body and the shivers subsided. He nodded, as if he'd seen the difference the cover had made, and went to the drinks cabinet where he poured two large glasses of brandy. He passed her a brandy balloon. "Drink this."

She held it to her face and narrowed her eyes against the pungent brandy fumes.

"It'll do you good," he said encouragingly. He was obviously under the false impression she'd never tasted brandy before. She took a small sip—it *was* good, the best—and then she took a much larger one. He raised an amused eyebrow. "You like brandy?"

She nodded. "My grandfather always kept the best. He was of the opinion that childhood should be as brief as possible."

"An unusual attitude. Particularly with a grand-daughter."

"He was an unusual man."

"Where is your family now? Can you go to them? I can take you there, if you wish?"

She paused as she remembered her grandfather—now passed away—and her remaining family, staying in their holiday home on Lake Lucerne. Waiting. Depending on *her* to make everything right with the estate. Not knowing that she'd made everything worse. She shook her head. "There's no-one who can help."

He sat on the chair opposite and reached over for her hands. "You're warmer already." He looked up into her eyes.

"Who are you, and who are you running from? I may be able to help."

Just the thought of this gorgeous man becoming embroiled in her problems, dirtying himself with a connection to the Russian, made her fearful. She had to get away. She couldn't involve him. "Look, I'm really sorry about this. But I shouldn't be here. I shouldn't involve you."

"Involve me? I think it's too late for regrets. I'm involved whether you like it or not." He rubbed her hands between his. "You *can* trust me, you know."

She knew it. She could see it in his eyes. She gave him a faint, rueful smile. "Trusting isn't my problem. I always trust too much."

"And I, too little, so we're perfectly balanced. Tell me about yourself. I don't even know your name."

She hesitated. She wouldn't give the name she was known by. It was too risky. "Aurora." She just stopped herself from adding her surname.

"Aurora," he repeated softly, as if savoring her name.

"Yes, afraid so."

"A beautiful name. Sleeping Beauty's name."

"Quite. A comic curse for someone who sleeps little and who has no interest in trying to look beautiful."

He frowned and stared at her in disbelief. She really didn't need to hear any comments about how she should wear make-up or about how she should have her hair styled. "But—"

"And you are?"

He nodded, smiling, understanding her interruption and respecting it. "Sahmir."

She extended her hand to hers. "Pleased to meet you Sahmir."

"And I'm very pleased to meet you, also. Now"—he sat

back and took a sip of his drink—"why don't you tell me what happened and I'll see what I can do to help?"

She took another sip of her rapidly diminishing brandy. "I'm... *involved*, with some powerful men. *A* powerful man. Just one, really. He'd brought me to Paris under false pretenses... I thought he was offering something I desperately want. But"—she grimaced—"he wasn't. Instead he wanted things from me... things I wasn't prepared to give." She bit her lip, not wanting to describe what exactly the Russian had wanted, what it was that he'd tried to take by force.

"It's okay."

She looked up suddenly, surprised at his grim tone, which had shown only gentle consideration up to now.

"You don't have to elaborate," continued Sahmir. "I can guess."

Without thinking, she rubbed her arm where finger-sized bruises marred her skin. He leaned forward and took her hand in his, pulling it free of the duvet. "And these bruises? This man caused them?"

She nodded and he rose and paced over to the window, his mouth grim, anger edging his movements. He stood looking out of the window. She shifted in her chair and followed his gaze out to the square.

Snow lay heavily on every available horizontal surface: from the top of the square-clipped limes to the trim on the dormer windows that peeped out from the grey slate roofs of the mansions opposite. It was like a perfectly symmetrical cake, delicately frosted especially for Christmas. Christmas—the time for peace and goodwill to all men. That was a joke.

"I'm sorry," he said without turning round to her. "I hate violence—in any shape or form—particularly to the vulnerable."

She was surprised by how strongly he'd reacted to her

words and waited for him to elaborate. But he didn't. Instead, the silence lengthened as he continued to look out the window.

"It's stopped snowing," he said at last.

She looked up at the scattering of stars. "It'll freeze tonight." She shivered at the thought of herself, outside. With nowhere to go, no money. She'd have died of exposure in the park.

He turned to her. "Are you still cold?"

She shook her head, swallowing back the fear. "No. It's just… I can't go out there again. I can't risk being seen by him again. He'll make sure I won't escape next time."

"There won't be a next time. Stay here. I can protect you."

She shook her head. What could this man do to protect her from people as evil as the Russian and his entourage? "No. I can't stay here. It's too close to him."

He frowned and walked up to her. "Who is he? Where does he live?"

"I can't tell you. It's too dangerous."

He plucked a phone from his pocket and dialed.

"Who are you calling?"

"The police. We'll let them deal with this."

She snatched the phone from his hands and pressed the screen, cutting off the dial tone. "No! I'm sorry, but no. He has friends everywhere. Even in the police."

"Who *is* this man?"

She shook her head. "It's best you don't know." She looked around, panicking once more. What the hell was she doing here? Not only was she endangering this man but, all the time she sat, lulled by the comfort of the brandy and fire, she wasn't putting space between her and the Russian. "I've got to go. Now!" She threw off the duvet and jumped to her feet.

"Where? You won't go to the police."

"A hotel. Where no-one knows me. It'll be better for me somewhere public."

"And then what?"

"I'll return to my family in Lucerne, get what I need and then go to ground in the country. I know of a place where he won't find me." She nodded, relieved to have come up with something of a plan. "That's what I'll do."

"If this man knows where your family is, I suggest you all go into hiding directly."

"I have no money, no clothes, no anything."

"You *can* stay here, you know."

She shook her head. "No. No, I can't."

"Okay, but let me help you." He walked over to his desk and picked up a wallet and plucked out a handful of notes. "Here." He handed it to her. "This will keep you going." He picked up his phone. "Tell me your account number and I'll have more money credited to your account immediately. Once you're out of Paris you can access these funds to set yourself up with whatever you need."

"But I can't pay you back. Not yet anyway."

"There's no need. I'm happy to help."

"Why?" she half-whispered, overcome by the generosity of this stranger.

"Because…" He looked away and shrugged. "Do I need a reason?"

"No, I guess not. It's just that it's so generous of you."

A single chime of a church bell rang out, pristine in the icy stillness.

He nodded to himself, as if coming to a decision. "I'll take you to the Ritz."

"Not the Ritz. Something smaller, something less showy, more discreet…"

"Somewhere where this man won't think to look."

She nodded. "Yes."

He took her hand and hesitated as he searched her face, for what, she had no clue. And for one long moment she had the notion that when he inclined his head to hers, he was going to kiss her. She swayed a little toward him, from pure instinct. But he stepped away.

"I hope, Aurora, that you evade this man, and will be able to stop running away. Running away is never the answer."

"Sometimes it is. When there's no place else to go, it is. Haven't you ever done that? Ever run, rather than face what you can't change, what you can't escape from any other way?"

He appeared to almost recoil at her words. He shook his head in a jerky motion that she took to be a negative response.

"You're lucky then." She looked around the room that was prepared for his imminent departure. "So, what takes you away from this beautiful house at Christmas? Family?"

"Sort of. I've spent many years based in Paris. But it's time to return home, back to the sun, to the light."

She gestured to the uncurtained window. "That's ironic. Just look how bright it is out there." He followed her gaze and looked out at a world clothed in an ethereal white glow.

She knew about heartache, knew about how you projected your own feelings onto the world. She turned and looked, really looked, at this charming, kind man with the devastating smile. He wasn't smiling now and she could see a story of pain in his eyes. "Perhaps it's not outside where it's dark." Anger flashed into his eyes as he turned back to her. And she stepped away. What the hell was she thinking? "I have to go. Could you call me a taxi?"

The anger was gone as soon as it appeared. But the smile didn't return. "I'll take you. I know of a place."

It was a short drive through the Paris streets to the small but exclusive hotel which Sahmir used occasionally when he needed to be discreet about his lovers.

He swung the car in front of the closed doors and turned off the engine. "The concierge will be here in a few moments."

She didn't answer, just sat looking anxiously up at the elegant facade. "Are you sure I'll be safe there?"

No he wasn't. But it was the only place he knew where a woman could buy a change of clothes, rest, and have a hire car waiting for her first thing in the morning.

"It's the best place I can think of. They've been discreet in the past about which Middle Eastern sheikh was sleeping with which Premier's married daughter."

She looked at him with those blue eyes, their color no longer visible in the dim interior of the car. But he knew their shade, not sapphire as he'd first thought, but something more delicate—like a rain-washed sky. "Are you that sheikh?"

The sound of a door being unbolted saved him from answering. He began to rise from his seat but she put out her hand to stop him. "Don't come out. I'm fine. You've done more than enough. You don't need to risk any more rumors about sheikhs with heiresses."

"And is that what *you* are?"

"Was." She smiled briefly. "Thank you so much. For everything."

She leaned forward and kissed his cheek. At the same time he turned to face her and their lips touched. It was brief but the effect was anything but. He felt her small gasp of surprise on his lips before she withdrew and he felt the same shock within himself. It was like the coming together of the opposite ends of a magnet. It just felt right.

"You're welcome. Maybe one day we'll meet under

different circumstances. And you'll wear that beautiful dress in the sunshine when you're happy."

"That'll never happen."

He frowned. "Why?"

"I always wear jeans. I dress to please myself, not anyone else."

"You never want to please anyone?"

"Not now. Not ever again."

She pulled away suddenly and was out of the car before he knew it. Instinctively he reached for her. She turned and, instead, he said, *"Bonne chance"*, and closed the door behind her.

He stayed only to watch her enter the lobby. Then he drove off into the night, back to his home. But only for tonight. He'd got what he'd come to Paris for—finance that secured his country's future. Now it was time to leave.

As soon as she entered the hotel lobby, Aurora knew she'd made a dreadful mistake. It was the quickly shifting eyes of the concierge, despite his otherwise neutral expression, which first alerted her. But it was after she was ushered into a small room beside the reception desk that she knew for sure.

The door closed with a too secure click and she turned to find the concierge hadn't followed her into the room. Then she stared in horror as the door opposite opened and the Russian entered the room.

He smiled a smile that sent chills washing through her body. She thought she was going to be sick, and it was only the refusal to humiliate herself in front of this man that stopped her. Sahmir had betrayed her. She'd trusted in someone yet again who'd betrayed her. He must have guessed where she'd come from and contacted the Russian when he'd gone to fetch the duvet.

"Rory."

"Vadim!" she said, her chin held high. "I'm staying here the night and then I'm leaving Paris."

He laughed and walked up close to her, trying to intimidate her by his height and heaviness. "No, my sweet, you won't be leaving Paris tomorrow. You're coming back with me."

CHAPTER 2

"Stand," said Sahmir, confirming his request for no more cards by sliding his cards under the pile of money. Vadim—or the Russian as he was more generally known—hadn't moved an inch. Sahmir had him worried, which was exactly what he wanted.

Sahmir glanced around the room. It wasn't his first visit to the small casino-hotel the Russian chose to use as his base when in Paris, but he'd never been to this private room before. Where was she? Behind one of the doors? The game had been going for hours and still she hadn't appeared. The Russian usually liked to show off his trophy women.

To think he nearly didn't contact the hotel this morning. If he hadn't, he wouldn't have pieced together what had happened—that the Russian also obviously used the hotel on a regular basis and had bribed the hotel's doorman more than Sahmir had. Nor would he have been able to arrange this last-minute game with the Russian.

Of all the people Aurora had to be involved with, it was *this* man—a man he'd first played cards with at university in

Paris, a man who'd turned into one of the most ruthless criminals in Europe.

"Hit." Sweat glistened on the Russian's forehead as he accepted a card from the dealer. He looked at it and swallowed. Sahmir knew the Russian had bust before he said it. He could tell by the pinching at the corners of the Russian's narrow eyes. He knew for sure when the Russian looked up at him with eyes that were as cold as they were angry. Sahmir took a leisurely mouthful of whiskey as they both waited for the dealer to deal his remaining cards.

One after another the dealer dealt to himself. "Bust," the dealer called, looking nervously at the Russian. No doubt the small casino relied heavily on the Russian's patronage and no doubt they lived in constant fear because of it. Sahmir pulled the winnings toward him. The dealer quickly left the room, his relief palpable.

The Russian's eyes glittered under the overhead light. "You're on fire tonight, my friend."

Sahmir hid his repugnance at being called the man's friend. He had to do something to bring her out. He knew the Russian's weaknesses, of which there were plenty, and he knew how to subtly goad the Russian into making the wrong move in cards. He'd try the same tactic now. "Run of luck, Vadim, that's all. Anyway, that's my last." He pushed his empty glass away. "I'll call it a night."

"It's still early."

"You call three a.m. early?"

"I do if my gambling partner is about to leave taking all the winnings and not giving me a fair shot at winning some back."

Sahmir felt the crackle of tension in the air. He'd been playing with fire for too long not to notice. Vadim was not a man to cross but he had no choice if he was going to find

CLAIMED BY THE SHEIKH

Aurora. He forced himself to smile. "I'm returning to Ma'in today."

"Of course. You're getting married, I understand. Some heiress from a neighboring country. Ugly as sin no doubt, but with money. And money talks, does it not? Tariq has it all sewn up, hasn't he? Tell me, Sahmir, what's it like to be at the beck and call of your older brother?" The Russian rose and accepted a light for his cigarette from one of his men, blowing the smoke casually into Sahmir's face.

Sahmir resisted the desire to turn away.

"What's it like being told to marry a woman you hardly know?" continued the Russian.

Sahmir gritted his teeth and smiled a mirthless smile. "It's all good," he eventually said when he could trust himself. He stood up and thrust the cash and banker's checks into his pockets.

"All good, indeed." The Russian drew deep on the cigarette, his eyes narrowing as he continued to stare at Sahmir. "Your heiress will bring you a lucrative sea port as well as more minerals than you can mine in a generation. You're a lucky man, indeed, not to mind who you sleep with in order to become wealthy."

"I hear you're partial to heiresses too."

"Indeed, but I have higher standards than you. Wealth, class *and* beauty are non-negotiable. A virgin is preferable, but they're so hard to find these days."

Sahmir huffed, disgusted to his core. "Of course, Vadim. Got yourself that French estate you've been wanting, I understand."

"Close. An estate in the Principality of Roche, near Monaco, to be exact. Got myself an heiress too. She's a true aristocrat. But an aristocrat with a temper"—he touched a cut on his lip—"but I'm working on that." He nodded to one of his bodyguards who promptly disappeared.

Sahmir felt sick to his stomach.

"Yes," the Russian continued, sucking on his Gauloises cigarette. "The estate is very beautiful. You must come and visit me there some time."

"Of course." Sahmir's words froze in his mouth as the door swung open and one of Vadim's men half-dragged in a woman, dressed in an evening dress he recognized instantly —deep red with a billowing skirt and a black bodice. She tossed her long dark hair back from her face, her chin defiant and eyes blazing. Eyes that he'd seen the night before —eyes the color of a rain-washed sky—with a swollen bruise the size of a fist, which he'd not seen the night before, on her cheekbone.

He swallowed back the rising bile and, looking away from her, brushed an imaginary fleck from his jacket. Years of hiding his feelings in front of his gambling opponents had stood him in good stead. Except it wasn't a winning hand he needed to hide now. He prayed she wouldn't reveal they'd met, otherwise he'd never get her out of here. And get her out of here, he would.

WHAT THE HELL was Sahmir doing here? The bastard! Rory glared around the room, daring anyone to speak, daring anyone to touch her again. But they weren't looking at her, they were looking at Sahmir. She returned her gaze to Sahmir and opened her mouth to speak but before she could say anything, the Russian was on her, his hands gripping her hair as he yanked her to face him and planted a kiss—a disgusting open-mouthed kiss—on her. She pulled away and spat at him. It landed on his cheek, hung there for a second, before he brushed it off in disgust and slapped her face. It stung, but no more than the humiliation.

She blazed another look at Sahmir. But the shock on his

face looked genuine and, for the first time, she wondered if he really had betrayed her to the Russian. His betrayal had haunted her all the night and long day. She'd trusted him instinctively and he'd surrendered her back to this monster. But now, confronted with his reaction which he'd quickly hidden from the others, doubt crept into her mind. She swallowed back the insults. Which was probably just as well because her voice was hoarse from screaming at the Russian.

"You see," said the Russian to Sahmir. "I told you she was a firebrand."

Sahmir slipped out of his jacket and with deliberate precision hooked it carefully onto the back of the chair before looking up at the Russian. "One more game then?"

The Russian laughed. "Ha! So you like the look of her?" He turned to Aurora. "This is Prince Sahmir ibn Saleh al-Fulan of Ma'in. A genuine sheikh, my darling. And this is Aurora Lucienne de Chambéry."

She narrowed her eyes. Why was the Russian introducing Sahmir to her? Surely he knew of their meeting the previous night? Had Sahmir somehow betrayed her while managing to keep his name out of it? Or maybe Sahmir *hadn't* betrayed her. Perhaps it had been a hotel employee who'd betrayed her? Whoever it was, she was certain the Russian didn't know she'd met Sahmir and, until she understood what was going on, she wasn't about to enlighten him.

But what about Sahmir? If only he'd meet her gaze, she felt she'd know if he was guilty of betrayal. Only one way to find out for certain. She'd test him.

She shook off the hand of the bodyguard and walked over to Sahmir. Sahmir appeared intent on spreading out an obscene pile of money in front of him. She extended her hand to him. He'd have to look up now and she'd know from his expression once and for all if he was guilty of betrayal.

His nostrils flared as she took another step closer, as if

breathing in her scent. Then he looked up abruptly and in that moment she knew. He'd had no idea. Somehow, he was mixed up with the Russian and it had nothing to do with her. His eyes were angry, disgusted and hurt all at the same time. But only she could see them. No-one else. He took her hand and squeezed it gently. "Aurora, pleased to meet you."

Hope leaped inside her. He'd get her out of here. Just as he'd tried to do last night, he'd do it tonight—rescue her from the Russian.

She stepped away as Sahmir turned another face to the others—an inscrutable face which revealed nothing but good humor and charm. How on earth could he go from what she saw in him, to this?

"Vadim, I think you're right. One last game. Winner takes all."

The Russian signaled to recall the dealer back into the room. His smug look of satisfaction made her glance back at Sahmir. What *was* his game?

"With a little variation. How about we spice it up a bit?"

"I'm listening," answered Sahmir quietly, his eyes intent and focused, his hands tapping the sheaf of notes onto the table, the only indicator of any agitation.

"One further game. Instead of bank drafts this time, I will use the lovely Aurora as my stake. One hand. One time. Do you accept?"

"No!" shouted Aurora.

The Russian didn't even look at her, just nodded his head in her general direction as if she were part of the furniture—a commodity to gamble with, something to trade.

Sahmir continued to tap, turn the pile of notes on their head, and then tap them again. He shrugged. "Really?"

"Yes, really. It would give me pleasure to know she was giving you pleasure." He turned to her. "And she needs to learn a little lesson about who's in control around here."

"Bastard!" This time the Russian turned and nodded to one of his men, who clamped a hand over her mouth.

Sahmir appeared not to notice. "Whatever you like."

"Whatever *you* like," grinned the Russian lasciviously. "Do you? Like her, I mean?"

Before she could move, he'd run his hand insolently over her breasts. She flinched and tried to move away but the bodyguard held her still. The Russian laughed. Sahmir hadn't watched, but kept his eyes firmly on the Russian.

"Yes, I like her. Who wouldn't?"

"Me, at the moment. I'd like her punished a little." The Russian sat forward and brushed his thumb heavily along the small cut on his lip. "She did this. A little punishment is in order. Let her know what she's really worth." He held up a gambling chip. "Nothing more than one of these. You're welcome to a night with her." He lifted crafty eyes to Sahmir. "If you win, that is."

Her face burned but she refused to say anything. Even when Sahmir shot her a glance that nearly killed her. She felt a huge lump rise in her throat. She wanted to cry—not rage-cry, not hate-cry—but pity-cry. She suddenly saw herself how he saw her.

"Good." The word was barely audible. Somehow Aurora knew that he'd meant to have spoken it louder. Sahmir cleared his throat. "The conditions are satisfactory. Let's begin." He nodded to the dealer who shuffled the cards.

The Russian sat opposite Sahmir. There were just the two of them, together with the terrified dealer, sitting at the large table. The Russian's men were ranged around the room, leaning against the wall, and Sahmir's own bodyguard stood behind him. He looked as if he could take them all on single-handed.

Aurora tried to shake off the firm grip of the bodyguard. The man grunted as Aurora kicked his shins and the Russian turned around and nodded to the bodyguard. "Let her be. She's not going anywhere." Then he glanced at Sahmir. "Not yet anyway."

Aurora sat quietly to one side, willing Sahmir to win. He was her *only* way out. She knew this now. She'd thought she could take on this Russian who'd inveigled his way into her father's life. She'd thought 'the arrangement' she'd been promised, which had lured her to Paris, would give her the right to remain on her estate. But the only arrangement the Russian had in mind was her signature to complete the legal transfer of the estate to him. And sex with her. Neither of which she'd given him.

She'd been a fool to come to Paris but she'd never heard of the *Solntsevskaya Bratva*, the Russian mafia, before and the last three days she'd seen and heard about things she'd always thought were tabloid inventions.

Only now did she realize just how innocent both she and her father had been and how utterly out of her depth she was with these criminals. But, for some reason, Sahmir knew them, and could deal with them.

Both men glanced at each other, eyes narrowed, no pretense at courtesy now. The rules of the game had been established and their focus was complete. There was no sound in the room except for the dull whirr of the air conditioner and the dealer shuffling the cards, the sound of the new pack crisp as they were fanned together and then separated, shuffled and then brought together again. No-one spoke. All eyes were focused on the cards that were being dealt.

Aurora shivered, unconsciously rubbing her bruised arm. Her whole body ached with the pain of the blows the Russian had dealt her, and a sleepless night of fear.

Sahmir pushed all his money in front of him, drew the cards toward him and flipped them up slightly to check them. He let them flick back to the table, face down, and pushed them under his money. "Stand."

"Confident, eh?" jeered the Russian.

"Of course. The size of my bet speaks for itself."

The Russian snorted. "I'd have accepted nothing less. Look at her. She's worth it."

But Sahmir didn't reply, he didn't even bother to look at the Russian.

The Russian nodded to a bodyguard who walked over to Aurora and tugged off one of her bracelets and gave it to the Russian. The Russian pushed it toward Sahmir. "I could have her lay across the table if you prefer?" He looked at her and her blood ran cold. How could she have underestimated this man? He was evil to the bone.

Sahmir looked up, his face grim. He didn't look at her. "The bracelet will suffice." He kept his gaze fixed on the Russian and for the first time, Aurora could see the steely depths in Sahmir. He appeared to be an entirely different character to the Russian, but she realized Sahmir would be equally formidable in a battle of wits. She just hoped to God, that any similarity ended there. Just hoped that he'd win, and that then she'd be free to disappear.

The Russian glanced at his cards and scraped them against the table. "Hit," he muttered. He didn't move for a moment, but continued to hold Sahmir's gaze. Then slowly he looked at the card the sweating dealer had pushed over to him.

Aurora could tell by the lack of movement from the Russian that he'd received a good card—good for him but bad for her and Sahmir. When he looked up his eyes were bright with excitement. Without moving his gaze from Sahmir he scraped his cards once more against the table, the sign for another card. "Hit."

Another card was pushed across to him. Another look of

smug satisfaction. Aurora felt sick. She glanced at Sahmir. But his expression hadn't changed. He betrayed nothing. She had no idea what he was thinking; no idea whether his hand was good or bad.

Again, the Russian scraped his cards against the table. "Hit," he mouthed, his eyes fixed on Sahmir. Another card was pushed across the table. The Russian's shoulders relaxed and he sat back in his chair, the relief visible.

"No!" Aurora called out.

The Russian turned to her sharply. "Shut her up!" he shouted at his bodyguard who clamped his hand across her mouth. She noticed that Sahmir's concentration hadn't wavered. The Russian turned once more back to the game, obviously annoyed at the distraction.

Was she really destined to stay with the Russian? Sahmir might have given her whereabouts away to the Russian. But somehow she didn't think so. That Sahmir mixed with people like the Russian suggested he wasn't a good man. But last night he'd *seemed* good, and infinitely better than the Russian. He'd listened to her, he'd been kind—neither things the Russian had been. She *had* to leave this room with Sahmir. She'd rather die than submit to the Russian.

Sahmir and the Russian exchanged a long look, neither revealing a thing. Would the Russian risk another card? If it took him over the magic number of twenty-one, he'd lose both a fortune and her. She didn't kid herself that he cared anything for her, only his pride. But he most certainly cared for the money that was heaped in front of Sahmir. The number of noughts on the Russian's bank check which lay casually on the top made her retch as her stomach reacted to the fear. The Russian wanted that money desperately and that meant he'd get her, too.

The Russian looked down at the back of his cards. He'd

not gleaned anything by looking at Sahmir, she could tell. His nerves were now showing in the nervous tic in his jaw and the grey gleam of sweat that beaded on his forehead and upper lip. His eyes rose back to Sahmir.

Aurora's heart was pounding so loudly she thought everyone would hear it. The Russian was going to win. There was no way the dealer or the casino would dare to interfere in the outcome of the game. It was between the Russian and Sahmir, and Sahmir was going to lose.

The Russian sat back in his chair. Would the Russian assume Sahmir had stopped because his two cards hit the magic number, in which case the Russian had to push forward and ask for another card? Or would he think Sahmir was bluffing, in which case he'd be best sticking with what he already had and not taking that extra risk?

Sahmir revealed nothing. He made no move. He sat, not slouching in his chair, but not ill at ease either. He looked perfectly composed. He must have nerves of steel, not to mention a heart of ice, to engage the Russian in this sort of game. If he won, was she jumping from the frying pan into the fire?

The Russian's hand flickered over the cards and then withdrew. He clicked his fingers and a lighted cigarette was given to him immediately. He sat back.

"What do you reckon, Sergei?" he asked his bodyguard behind him, breaking all the rules of the game by talking to his men. It seemed everything was to be on his terms. "Is the sheikh bluffing?"

The bodyguard knew better than to answer. He remained silent, gripping Aurora's arms.

"Huh?" The Russian leaned forward and narrowed his eyes, blowing smoke into Sahmir's face. Sahmir's bodyguard flexed his hands but didn't move. Sahmir waited one moment and then slowly moved forward, arms crossed on the table in front of him.

"Do you want me to tell you?" Sahmir asked.

"It would certainly make life easier."

"It would only make life easier for you, if you knew whether I was lying or not."

The Russian inhaled heavily on his cigarette. A pall of smoke lay over the table, the electric light catching its movement. "Tell me."

"I'm bluffing." Sahmir sat back. No smile, no grimace, nothing but a steely intensity. His face was eerily shadowed from the overhead light. He looked nothing like the man she'd met the previous night.

"A double bluff." The Russian blew out smoke but it was bravado. He was losing his nerve. She could see it in the quick movement of his eyes.

Sahmir said nothing.

The Russian didn't try to wipe away the sweat that trickled from his brow. He scraped his cards against the table once more. "Hit."

The dealer slid the card along to him face down. Her life depended on a game of chance. Surely Sahmir wouldn't leave her here? Maybe he'd call the police and they'd come for her. But she knew in her heart that wouldn't happen. They'd be gone, have left this place, before help arrived.

Suddenly the Russian's hand shot out and partly lifted the card. He stared at it as if he couldn't believe it. He turned over the cards to reveal a bust hand. It all depended on Sahmir's cards now.

Sahmir turned his cards over with deliberate precision. One ace and a three. If the Russian had stopped on his fourth card, he'd have won. Sahmir had indeed been bluffing.

All eyes were on the dealer as he turned over cards that led to an inevitable bust.

"My game, I think." Sahmir stretched forward and plucked the bracelet from the middle of the table and cast a quick look at Aurora. For the first time she could see his relief. Was it for the money, or for her?

But before Sahmir could move his hand, the Russian's large hairy hand clamped over Sahmir's. "Why the haste my friend? You would not do me out of the chance to win her back, surely?"

"You've had your chance and you lost. Didn't your mother ever tell you that when the party's over, it's over?"

The Russian scowled dangerously. "One more time." He glanced at the money.

Sahmir gripped the bracelet and sat back, tapping the gold bangle against his other hand. "I'll tell you what I'll do. As a measure of my good will." He pushed the notes to the Russian and scooped up the rest of the cash and shuffled it on the table in front of them all. "Keep the bank's promissory notes. They're always such a hassle to cash."

Sahmir rose and thrust the cash into his pocket. "And I'll keep my night with Aurora." He turned to her and offered her the bracelet. "Yours I believe?"

Aurora tried to pull herself away from the bodyguards but their grip was still tight. "Let me go!"

"I'd do as she asks, if I were you," Sahmir said so quietly and yet so firmly that the bodyguard released her. Sahmir extended his hand to her and she hesitated. He smiled, the warm, coaxing smile of the night before, and she stepped toward him. She had no choice. He was her only way out.

The Russian scowled again but this time at Aurora. "Give her to the sheikh."

Aurora was suddenly thrust toward Sahmir and he caught her, steadied her but revealed nothing in his eyes which were trained steadily on the Russian. Sahmir was still in absolute control. "We'll be leaving."

"No, you won't. You want her, you have her *here*"—the Russian nodded to an adjoining room—"or not at all."

Sahmir's bodyguard stepped forward, filling the small space with his massive physique. Sahmir held up his hand to stop him.

"You surely wouldn't renege on the bet?"

"Of course not. I'm a man of honor." The Russian smiled slyly. "If you want her you can have her. Out the back. Now. And then leave."

"And what if I want to take her with me?"

"When you leave, you leave alone. If you want her, you have her here."

"Then I want the night. Not just a half-hour."

The Russian shrugged. "That's fine. So long as she doesn't leave. I'm not letting her get away again. Not until I've got what I want from her. I'll have my men placed outside."

Sahmir shrugged. "No need for that. I'll keep her too busy to think about escaping."

The Russian grinned. "Fine. Go now, you can use that room."

Sahmir took hold of her hand firmly, reassuringly, and didn't let it go.

"You seem to like the look of the sheikh, Aurora," said the Russian suspiciously. "I didn't wager you for your benefit." He looked from one to the other as Sahmir shot her a quick glance. She tried to tug her hand away in a show of reluctance. And then again harder but Sahmir gripped her more tightly.

"That's better," said the Russian, reassured that he wasn't giving her pleasure. "Now go. Enjoy yourself."

Sahmir, his grip still firm around Aurora's wrist, walked over to his bodyguard and said a few casual words. The man left immediately.

He took her to the room indicated and pulled her inside. The beautifully furnished room was a mess of broken glass and spilled wine and food. At its center was an unmade bed with ropes dangling from the bedstead.

He let her go and walked quickly from window to window, signaling to someone outside. "Aurora? Get your bag."

She nodded and ran to the open wardrobe and picked up her backpack leaving behind her bulky suitcase. "How the hell are we going to get out?"

He brought his finger to his lips and jerked his head to the window. "That's the only way." He walked up and whispered into her ear. "Any good at sounding as if you're having sex against your will, when you're not having sex at all?"

She almost sobbed with relief, now that she'd had her suspicions confirmed—Sahmir wasn't about to rape her. She nodded and gave a tentative cry.

"Louder," he whispered.

She gave another gut-wrenching cry, summoning all of her fear and loathing from the past week. Anyone outside could well imagine she was being subjected to things she didn't want.

Sahmir nodded and went to the window once more and peered out. They were a couple of floors above ground level and the back room looked out onto a service alleyway. The once grand house had been transformed into a commercial property, and other buildings had been built on the rear garden.

Aurora made a further cry, followed by a convincing sob when she saw Sahmir's bodyguard had brought reinforcements into the alley. She realized what Sahmir was about to do and let out a prolonged wail during which Sahmir lifted the sash window high and indicated she should climb out.

The ground seemed a long way away but there was a sturdy drainpipe which ran down the side of the window. She could see at a glance that its disrepair would work in her favor. There would be plenty of footholds.

"Can you climb down that?" he whispered into her ear.

She nodded, thanking God for those summers of tree climbing on the estate. She sat on the windowsill, swung her legs over, and reached out for the drainpipe, clinging tightly to it as she leaped so her feet landed on the joint of the pipe. It was freezing cold but she had no time to worry about that. Instead she focused on shifting her hands and feet carefully down the drainpipe.

After several minutes she looked up and Sahmir hissed one word at her. "Jump." She gasped and looked down. There was still a drop, but Sahmir's bodyguard stood waiting at the bottom, arms outstretched. They were running out of time. She had no choice. She took a deep breath, let herself go into the darkness and was caught by strong arms. Her backpack followed her seconds later. Then Sahmir dropped to the ground.

The lights of a car across the road flashed and they walked quickly over to it, Sahmir pushing Aurora into the back of the car, following in behind while the two bodyguards took the wheel and the passenger seat.

Aurora curled up on the seat, instinct keeping her low.

The car started immediately and crept away, with no headlights until it reached the end of the street when it tore off down the boulevard.

She was shaking with shock. Once more Sahmir took off his jacket and covered her with it. "Where are we going?"

"To the airport."

"I want to go home. Please. Let me go home to my mother and sister."

"Why? Do you really want the Russian to find you?"

"No, I want to go—"

He took her chin in his hand and brought her face sharply around to face him. If he'd been inscrutable at the gambling table, he was showing enough emotion now. He was incredulous. "There's no *way* you, your mother or sister can ever go back home now. Not unless you want to end up with the Russian again."

"But I have nowhere else to go." She looked out the window at the streets that sped by. They must have been traveling at twice the speed limit. "Where are we going?"

"To the airport. To board a plane to my country. Do you have your passport in your bag?"

She nodded, dumbly.

"Good, that will make things easier. Without it, I'd have to have called in a few favors. With it, we can be in the air, on the way to Ma'in more quickly."

"We're leaving France, leaving Roche." She couldn't hide the misery she felt at leaving her country, her estate, the only place she'd ever called home.

"Don't you understand, Aurora?" he said impatiently. "You gambled coming to Paris to see the Russian. You gambled and you lost." He looked at her pityingly. "You lost," he repeated "more than you imagined you would."

She realized he thought the Russian had raped her.

"He didn't, you know, do the things—"

"I don't want to know," he interrupted. "You don't have to tell me anything." Sahmir sat back heavily and looked out the front window, his features colorless and tense under the flashing orange of the passing lights. She felt soiled, she felt the victim that he must see her as.

"He didn't do anything, sexually…" She looked out the black window… at nothing. "He couldn't. It seems that talking was all he could do." She couldn't prevent the sob from rushing up through her body. It was only stopped by his hand which he gently placed over hers. He still didn't look at her, just focused on the road ahead.

"Try to forget. It's over."

She looked ahead of her, at the overhead signs that showed they were close to the airport.

Over? It had only just begun.

CHAPTER 3

*A*ll the way to the airport, Sahmir was on the phone, talking in a language she couldn't understand, with an urgency she did.

She half-listened, trying to guess the instructions he issued, trying to work out where on earth she was going. Deep down, she hardly cared. She'd got away from the Russian. She'd got away from him, she repeated to herself, closing her eyes against the blur of lights as they sped along the motorway. She suddenly felt exhausted and fell back into the jacket Sahmir had put around her shoulders, breathed in his aftershave and closed her eyes.

"Aurora, we're here." Sahmir's voice was a welcome intrusion on her dreams.

She blinked. "Where?"

"Charles de Gaulle airport."

"Oh." She rubbed her eyes, hoping it would help clear her head. It didn't. She still felt as if she was dreaming. It was only when she stepped outside onto the tarmac that the cold cleared her confusion.

"It's nearly morning." She stood outside the car, looking around at the slowly awakening airport—lit and full of people, even at that early hour. She breathed deeply of the frigid, fresh air. She felt as if she'd been inhaling strong cigarette smoke and stale whiskey for years. But it had only been a few days since she'd arrived in Paris.

"Come on. Not much further before you can rest properly."

It was only the promise of sleep that made her put one leaden foot in front of the other, and the support of the bodyguard on one side and Sahmir on the other. Somehow she managed to get through passport control, with the officials bowing and scraping before Sahmir, in a way she'd never before experienced. But Sahmir didn't take advantage of it, and was unfailingly polite and charming. It was only after they'd completed the formalities and were walking out onto the tarmac, toward the steps that led to a small jet, that she could see the strain in his face. Under the bright lights of the airport lights that flooded the runway, he looked tense, his mouth grim.

They were greeted at the foot of the steps by the co-pilot. As soon as they'd run up the steps, the doors were closed and the plane began to move.

Aurora walked through a strangely empty space, filled only with comfortable settees and a coffee table, and took the seat shown to her, while Sahmir spoke with the pilot and the other staff. He disappeared briefly, only returning to his seat just as the plane turned on the tarmac and the bright jewel-like lights of the runway stretched out in front of them.

"Are you okay?" He brought a wad of material to her face and she wriggled back, fumbling with her seat belt.

"No!" Had she been wrong about him? Was he about to drug her now?

He moved away and raised his hands to show her what he was holding. "It's an ice pack, Aurora. An ice pack. I'm neither going to hit you over the head with it, nor clamp it to your mouth."

She opened her mouth to speak but instead, she felt tears threaten and she closed her mouth, blinking madly.

"It's for your cheek." He offered it to her and she took it and held it in place, glad of the chill against her heated face.

"Thank you," she whispered, trying to control the mounting tension.

He sighed. "I'm so sorry. I should never have let you go last night. If I'd known it was Vadim you were running from. Known *he* was the man you were involved with—"

"Involved with?" Anger rescued her from breaking down. "I'm only 'involved' because he and his lawyers tricked me into coming to Paris to meet him! Apparently the estate isn't legally his until I sign some papers. That's why they brought me to Paris. Not to give me back my estate—but to take it from me, once and for all."

"Aurora, please, don't distress yourself. It's over."

"Not for me, it's not." She could feel the tears pricking once more at her eyes. She closed them tight. "Not for me. Without my signature he'll never leave me alone."

The plane ascended sharply then and she realized they'd left the ground, left Europe— the only land she'd ever lived in, the only home she'd ever known. "What's the name of your country?"

"Ma'in."

"Ma'in?" She racked her brains, trying to remember what she'd heard about it. "I think I've heard of it. A small country in the Middle East?"

"That's the one. My brother is King of Ma'in. You'll be safe there."

Afterwards she realized it was the relief that did it. The tears that had been threatening didn't come when she was being bullied, didn't come when she was being insulted or when she was fighting, they only came when she really believed she was safe.

And they came noisily. She rarely cried, and when she did it wasn't pretty crying like she'd seen in the movies. All she could do was sit with the palms of her hands flat against her eyes, howling, as tears streaked from her hands and ran down her face.

They didn't stop easily and many minutes passed before the pressure of emotion eased and she tried to wipe the tears away with her hands.

He didn't attempt to touch her, just passed her a wad of tissues. She wiped her eyes, blew her nose and sat back.

"Aurora, are you okay?"

She shook her head. "Not Aurora. Rory. My family calls me Rory." The thought that she'd just left her country with a man who didn't even know her name made her break down again.

"Rory, are you okay?" he asked, after she'd cried the tears out of her, and her body was hiccupping for air like a toddler after a tantrum.

He angled his face in front of her so she could see him, although she sat looking straight opposite. He pushed aside her tangled hair. "I don't know what happened to you and I don't want to know. But I want you to know that you're safe with me. I'll never let anyone hurt you. Don't be upset."

"I'm not," she hiccupped, unable to see him through the tears that had sprung up again. "I'm not crying because I'm scared of you."

"Then why the tears? Why now?"

It took a few minutes before the sobbing subsided again. "I don't know. Oh, God," she said as she wiped her eyes once more. "I never cry. I'm always the strong one."

"You've every right to cry. It's not every week a woman is abducted by a Russian mafia boss and ends up leaving her country with a strange sheikh!"

She burst out laughing, just as he'd meant her to do, and then the laughter turned to tears once more. "That would be funny if it weren't all true," she said eventually. She suddenly felt exhausted. She lay back on the chair and rolled her head on the headrest to look at him.

He sat forward, his arms resting on his legs, his head forward looking at her, his eyes full of concern.

"I'm crying," she continued, "because you're the first man who's been nice to me for a long time."

"I'm sorry to hear that."

"No," she held up her hand. "Don't say lovely things like that. You'll only get me started again."

"I can't say lovely things to you?"

"Not yet. Maybe later, but not now. But thank you, for everything. I don't know where I'd be without you. Or rather I do, and I'm so grateful to you that I'm not there."

"I'm just sorry I couldn't help sooner." He raised his hand and gently touched her bruised cheek. "I could have saved you this. Here"—he passed her the ice pack—"it might be too late, but put this on. It should ease the pain and swelling."

She placed it against her cheek. It seemed to have no effect but it pleased Sahmir and she wanted to please Sahmir because she knew she'd never be able to repay him for what he'd done for her. "That's better," she lied. "Thank you again."

"Tell me, Rory, what on earth were you doing with the Russian in the first place?"

"It's a long story."

"It's a long flight. We have all night."

She didn't say anything to begin with, just looked out the window as they ascended through the clouds. She cleared her throat and turned back to him.

"My father died just over a week ago." Just saying the bleak words brought back the flood of emptiness and loss and anger. Anger that her father had tossed away his life, the love of his family and his estate on the fall of the dice.

"I'm sorry. Was it sudden?"

"Yes. He killed himself. He'd lived apart from us for some time. It was only when he'd died that we discovered the extent of his gambling problem."

"What was his name?"

"Jean-Paul de Chambéry. Why, did you know him?" She looked up at him suddenly but he was rubbing his eyes with the palms of his hands and didn't catch her eye. He suddenly looked exhausted.

"I don't know all the gamblers in Paris," he said after a long pause.

She sat back in her seat. "No, of course not. Anyway, turned out he'd been using the estate to raise money to feed his gambling habit. Senlisse has been in our family for ten generations. It means everything to me. I've been running it virtually single-handed the past few years. I've always loved it. And I was meant to have inherited it. I have just one younger sister, and my mother has no real interest in it." She sighed and fiddled with her fingers. "But it didn't happen like that."

"Go on."

"The first I knew of his death was when the Russian's men came and threw me off the estate. There was only me there, thank goodness. My mother and sister were at our holiday home in Lucerne. I was out checking on some repairs that were being done to the barn. When I returned, I walked in through the back door, from across the fields, so I had no idea. Then I heard voices from the formal part of the chateau and I walked through. The lawyers were there. I couldn't believe it when the lawyer told me what had happened. They told me the Russian now owned the estate. They even showed me papers that looked legal, stating the change in ownership." She sighed and shook her head. "And they told me the Russian wanted to meet me in Paris to come to some sort of 'arrangement' as regards the estate. They intimated that it would be in my interests to go. I had no choice. So I went there and I discovered the only arrangement he was interested in was forcing my signature on legal papers to complete the transfer of ownership."

"The Russian's been wanting the respectability of an estate for a long time. He's probably been grooming your father to that end for years."

"Respectability? Surely there were other ways he could get that? Marry, settle down, have children. Stop breaking the law."

He huffed a half-laugh. "He isn't about to do that, nor any of the other things that his family make their money through—drugs, prostitution, people smuggling. No, your estate was the key to respectability."

"And he needed my signature for that—not that he got it." She was silent for a few moments as she fiddled with her fingers. "You know, something else happened while I was with him. Something which showed me the kind of man I was dealing with."

Sahmir frowned. "What happened?"

"I think, I can't be sure, but I think, I saw him kill someone. It all happened very quickly. The guard had left the door open, I couldn't get away, not the way I'd been left." She shot an awkward look at Sahmir.

"Go on."

"I'd heard them talk about some big meeting. Something

about how they had 'him'—whoever 'he' was—where they wanted him. Then I heard Russian being spoken—at least it sounded like Russian to me—followed by a scuffle, shouting and then a horrible silence. Then I saw Vadim walk away with a knife. I swear there was blood on it."

Sahmir stiffened, suddenly serious. "Did he see you?"

She pressed her lips together to stop them from trembling and nodded. "I didn't see him actually stab anyone, just heard the noise, just saw him walk away."

"But did he believe you saw him kill someone?"

She met his serious gaze and nodded. "Possibly. I don't know."

He sat back in his seat. "I doubt you'd still be alive if he thought you'd seen him."

"Yes, of course." She sat back feeling reassured.

"Don't worry. You're safe now."

"Thank goodness. He's an evil man."

"Nothing's enough for a man like Vadim. He wants what he can't have, whether by deceit or violence. And he usually gets it."

She shook her head in disbelief. "You know all these things about him and yet you still gamble with him?" A shadow of doubt flitted through her mind. After all, she hardly knew Sahmir. "What on earth were *you* doing with the Russian?"

"I'm not a part of the mafia, if that's what's worrying you. There was a dark time in my life when I spent much of my time gambling... with people like the Russian. I'd thought those days were over until recently when we met up again over the gambling tables. He wanted another game and I'd declined. It was only when I discovered from the hotel that *he* was the man who you'd left with, that I changed my mind."

"I'm sorry if you lost money."

"I didn't. I rarely do. Besides, I think I received the better end of the deal."

Alarm bells went off in Rory's mind once more. "You do?"

He narrowed his eyes in that sexy way he had. "I do."

She frowned and looked down at her hands. Did he really imagine he'd won something permanent at the gambling table? Did he really think she was his, now? Or maybe it was simply a turn of phrase?

"Are you hungry?"

She shook her head. She *had* been, but any hunger had just vanished. "I'm fine."

"Something to drink? A coffee, brandy maybe? I remember how you like brandy," he added with a smile.

"It's six o clock in the morning."

"Seriously, I think you could do with it. You've had a hell of a time." He caught her gaze and her skin goose-bumped under his casual glance. "And, besides, you're still in your ball gown."

She pulled his jacket further around her, trying to hide her breasts that were too easily seen above the low-cut bodice. "Thanks for the reminder. And I think you're right. A small brandy would be good."

He rang for a brandy and as it was being poured out, the seat belt sign was switched off. He rose and held out his hand to her. "Come over to the lounge. You'll be more comfortable there. Unless you'd like to go to bed?"

Where the blush came from, Rory couldn't have said. His meaning was clear—he simply wanted to know if she needed to sleep—but for some reason her thoughts strayed to other things. Like the smell of his body close to hers the previous evening when he'd lifted her into his arms. Like the way his shirt hung on broad shoulders and his sleeves were pushed up untidily, revealing well-muscled arms. Like the way his eyes spoke a language all of their own, held a mischievous charm that he tried hard to suppress but was still revealed in the sparkle in his eyes. They were light with humor now in response to her blush.

"No, I don't want to go to bed." She shook her head and dragged her eyes from his. "No, thank you," she said dipping her head to look out the window, as if there were something of intense interest there.

He lowered his head, so he was beside her. "Something fascinating out there?"

She huffed a laugh and closed her eyes briefly. "Clouds." She turned to him and he was so close, so she could see his dark eyelashes framing eyes that were indecently sexy.

"You like clouds?"

"My mother always said I had my head in them. Now she's right."

He smiled. "You need to contact your family. They also need to go to a safe place, where Vadim won't find them. Can you think of somewhere?"

She nodded. "When I was a child we had some wonderful holidays in St Malo. We've no connections with anyone—they'll be safe there."

"Good." He passed her pen and paper. "Write down their contact details and I'll make the arrangements. Look, why don't you go and call your mother and then change? It might make you feel a little more comfortable."

The only thing that would make her feel more comfortable would be to not *be trapped on a private jet with a man she'd only known two days.*

"Sure," was all she said. She unclipped her seat belt with a shaking hand. She suddenly felt sick. Sick, tired and afraid. She rose and looked around. They were alone in the lounge, seated in cream leather chairs close to the cockpit. Beyond were more chairs, a long settee and a walnut dresser. "Down

CLAIMED BY THE SHEIKH

this way I guess," she said, trying to brush off her discomfort with humor.

"Yes, I don't think you'll get lost." He smiled reassuringly. "My valet will have put away your things."

She blushed at the thought of someone looking at the contents of her backpack. She'd had to leave her large suitcase with her smart 'city' clothes behind. Her backpack only contained a spare pair of jeans and a t-shirt They were clean but *very* well worn. Despite the estate, the land and four hundred-year-old chateau, she'd never had much money. Which was fine for a tomboy, fine for someone who lived her life in rubber boots, with horses, but not fine for someone jetting around the world in the company of a sheikh. "Right." She smiled, unsure, and walked past the dining room, through a study and into the bedroom. Sure enough, inside the wardrobe, a pair of much-washed jeans was neatly folded alongside a t-shirt and a sweater that had belonged to her father.

She told herself not to worry. Her mother was full of sayings and one of her favorites was 'count your blessings'. So she did. One, she was alive, two, she was safe, three, her mother and sister were safe. She looked to where Sahmir was checking out a computer screen and talking into his phone in the office. She couldn't hear him above the drone of the plane, but she could see him. And she felt a blast of that same attraction she'd felt when she'd first met him. Four—she really didn't need a four, but she had to admit a blessing she felt so strongly—she'd met Sahmir.

She closed the door and fell back against it and took a deep breath. She liked him. She *really* liked him. He'd saved her life and honor for God's sake. Then she looked at the bed. One bed. A large king size bed, it dominated the room and, as she turned to the bathroom, the bed also dominated her thoughts. She might like him but she didn't know him at all, and hadn't the first idea what he wanted from her. And, after what she'd been through, following up on an attraction was the last thing she wanted to do. Particularly if he felt he'd earned it.

Phone Maman first, she told herself. Then shower and dress and return to Sahmir and ask the question that loomed large in her mind—what the hell were they going to do?

HAVING FIRST ALARMED and then reassured her family, Rory turned her attention to herself.

It took longer than normal to shower, wash her hair and get changed. She never usually blow-dried her hair but, dressed in her ancient jeans and her father's old sweater to cover her worn t-shirt, she knew she needed to do something to try to fit in with her surroundings. But, a quarter of an hour later, she stood in front of the mirror and wondered why she'd bothered. She sighed.

Cautiously she emerged. Sahmir was at his desk. He turned and grinned at her, checking her out as he did so. "You look...more comfortable."

"I know." She swept her hands over the faded jeans and pulled her sweater over the hole that was growing on the worn part that covered her butt. "Not exactly clothes to wear on a private jet, I'm afraid."

He shrugged. "You look fine to me." Before she could react to his admiring glance, he continued. "Come and eat. You'll feel even more comfortable with food inside you."

She sincerely doubted that but followed him to the table anyway.

The dining table was spread with the freshest of French patisseries and strong coffee. She hadn't realized she was so hungry until that moment. He pulled out a chair for her at the dining table and a steward appeared from the rear of the

CLAIMED BY THE SHEIKH

plane and poured the coffee. While she ate, Sahmir sat back and observed her.

She ate in silence for a few minutes as she tried to summon courage to ask the question she needed to know the answer to. The only thing that was making her hesitate was a fear that she might not like his answer.

"Why are you frowning?"

She put down the knife she'd been using to cut up her croissant. "Why? Because I'm wondering about something. You said before that you thought you'd won the better deal. Better than what looked to be a small fortune. Tell me, Sahmir, what exactly do you think you've won?"

RORY'S QUESTION roused Sahmir from his reverie. He'd been admiring the way the bright sunlight that streamed in from the window, brought out the radiant red streaks in her hair. He'd not noticed them before. Her hair was even glossier now it had been straightened, even inexpertly, and he was tempted to run his finger down its sleek length. As she spoke, his eyes turned to her lips, so softly pink and inviting. He sighed and looked up into her eyes which were stern. "I've won the company of a beautiful woman for a short time."

The stern expression became sterner. "Well, lucky you. And by the word 'won' do you think you now own me?"

"Of course not." He rose, partly in order to appreciate her beauty better, and also to try to calm her, just as he'd calm an Arab mare out in the desert—a wild mare, one who didn't want to be captured. "I'm not the Russian."

"Maybe not. But as of a few hours ago, you're a man who's taken control of my life." She was testing him, probing him, wanting to find out just the kind of man she'd found herself bound up with.

"Not control, Rory. Never control. I have no interest in

controlling anyone. I have everything I need, everything I could want. When you are able to leave, you leave. It's as simple as that."

"And when do you think that will be?"

"That depends on what advice I receive from my lawyers. I've asked them to look into your affairs—I hope you don't mind—and report back to us." He paused, not wanting to tell her that he was also having the possible killing of another Russian investigated—she was frightened enough already. "In the meantime I suggest you enjoy a stay in Ma'in."

She nodded. "Thank you for all you're doing. But are you sure you don't mind? The Russian said you were about to be married. I can't imagine your fiancée will be pleased."

He shrugged. "It's an arranged marriage, we're not in love."

"That just sounds weird to a westerner. You didn't mind agreeing to an arranged marriage?"

"The western impression of an arranged marriage is often a very cynical one. It doesn't *have* to be all bad; it often *isn't* like that. The people who arrange it know the couple involved and have their best interest at heart."

"And, in your case, the country's."

"That is indeed so."

"Will she mind?"

"Who?"

"The woman you are to marry. Will she mind about… what's happened?"

"I doubt it. Besides, you're just a friend I'm helping out for a little while. Where's the harm in that?"

"You'd know better than me. But what if your lawyers aren't able to sort out the estate? I have to rejoin my family; I can't stay with you indefinitely."

It felt as if someone had snatched his breath away, taken away something he was meant to have. And *there*, in *that* moment, he knew he couldn't let her go. He let a few moments lapse, as he strove to be casual. Anything else would make her run a mile as soon as they landed.

"Then I have a few other ideas we can pursue. In the meantime, there's no need to rush away, to endanger yourself. My marriage is a quite separate issue. It won't be affected by your presence."

"Are you sure?"

He smiled. "I'm sure. Of course you can leave whenever you wish, as I've said. But I think it would be best for you to lay low in Ma'in until we've sorted out the situation. He wants you to sign those papers. And, knowing him, he won't stop until he finds you. Our job is to make him not need to find you. And, in the meantime, to keep you safe."

"How long do you think it'll take? A month or so?"

"Could be longer. You can stay as my guest in Ma'in, at the palace for as long as you need to."

She stood up—her nearly threadbare jeans hugging her slim hips and rousing his libido, affecting his body just when he needed to retain a cool focus.

"Surely there must be somewhere else in the world I can go where you won't have to be bothered with me."

"You're no bother. Stay. Treat it like a holiday. Now rest. You look tired."

She tried to stifle a yawn and failed. "One month then. No strings?"

He knew what she was asking. "No strings."

A steward appeared. "Sir, your brother would like a word."

"Of course." He rose and stretched. "Excuse me. I have to tell my brother that I'll be arriving shortly at Ma'in. I might just neglect to tell him that I'm bringing with me a woman who is not the woman I'll be marrying." He grinned ruefully. "I believe my fiancée-to-be won't bat an eyelid, but my brother most certainly will. He's old-fashioned like that. I think I'd better delay this particular piece of news until I arrive."

"I'm sorry I got you into this."

"It was my choice to act, Rory. Don't worry." He began to walk away and then turned, an unreadable smile on his lips. "We've another six hours until we land. Why not go to bed?"

She blushed. "I'm fine."

He was beginning to realize that she was one stubborn woman. He liked that. "Then use these controls to recline the chair." She pressed them, lay back and looked out the window.

When he returned, coffee in hand, Rory was lying, unmoving, facing away from him. "Rory, would you like a coffee?"

She didn't answer. He touched her arm gently and repeated the question. She still didn't answer. He leaned forward to see her better. She was fast asleep.

He smiled and turned back to the steward. "A cover please. And pull down the shades."

After the steward had dimmed the lights and left the room, Sahmir sat looking at Rory.

He could pinpoint precisely when he'd known Rory was someone special. It was the moment in the park that he'd leaned over to help her up from the snowy ground. She'd looked at him and he'd felt an instant connection. Not that he could do anything about it, he reminded himself. He was engaged to be married to a woman he didn't love. But they had a month. A month to enjoy each other's company... only in a platonic sense, of course.

He took the duvet and laid it gently over her.

She was lying on her side, with her hip uppermost. The worn jeans had a hole revealing the olive skin of her thigh.

He inhaled through gritted teeth. He looked at the exposed flesh for one long second, every part of him urging him to touch it, to kiss it. Instead he pulled the covers over her, hiding her. He'd promised to keep her safe and that's exactly what he'd do. Both from the Russian and himself. And he knew which one would be harder.

CHAPTER 4

It was the lack of movement that awoke her. The endless drone of the airplane had given way to a light hum and the plane was motionless. Slowly she opened her eyes and looked out the window, squinting against the bright light. After the short days and soft light of Paris, this light had the brilliance of a light seen through a prism—sparkling, almost overpowering.

She had no idea how long she'd been asleep but she hadn't moved. She was still in the same fetal position, curled up on her side on a chair that had been extended beneath her to make her more comfortable.

She looked around—there was no-one close. She could hear people moving in the next room, and the pilot talking to ground control, so they hadn't been here long. She stretched and winced as she felt the painful throb of her cheekbone. Despite that, she felt a lot better. The events of the past week were already beginning to recede like a nightmare.

She propped herself up and looked out at the airport hangar, long and low and white under a brilliant blue sky. *Ma'in*. A country she'd only heard of from obscure TV travel programs on those evenings when she'd been exhausted after spending all day riding out on the estate, working alongside the farm workers to get crops in before the weather turned.

She racked her brains trying to remember what the presenter had talked about. Gold mines, maybe? Certainly wealthy. Or at least in recent years. And she'd somehow ended up as guest of the royal family. She'd have found it funny if she'd known how to extricate herself. But there was no way she could do that without putting herself in danger. Hopefully in one month's time she'd be returning to Europe free of the specter of the Russian. In the meantime all she had to be was a model guest for Sahmir.

She owed Sahmir; she owed him a lot.

She rose and went to the bathroom, splashing cold water on her face and brushing her hair. It was warm now that the air conditioning was tempered by the hot air flowing in through the open door of the plane and she slipped out of her jersey, tying it around her waist. She was about to leave when she glanced in the mirror and saw to her horror that the worn bra and t-shirt had made them both almost see-through. She pulled the jersey from around her waist and slung it around her shoulders instead, tying it loosely around her chest. It was the best she could do. When she returned to the lounge, Sahmir was waiting for her.

"Good morning! How are you feeling?"

She pulled a face, suddenly feeling awkward. "I feel like I'm sleepwalking and someone will wake me up soon from this dream."

"At least it's a dream and not a nightmare any more." He gestured for her to precede him. "Come, the car's waiting."

"My stuff. I'd better go and pack."

"It's been taken care of. Your backpack is in the car already. We've been waiting for you to awake."

"You delayed your departure for me?" She walked up to

the open door, down which a flight of steps descended to the tarmac, shimmering in the heat.

"It wasn't a problem. I've been working in the study and I wasn't expected to arrive here until later in the week. Besides, you'd been through a lot and were exhausted."

She paused on the top step, frowning. "Are you always like this?"

"Like what?"

"So considerate."

He grinned. "Only with women I've claimed from their kidnappers."

She didn't return his grin but proceeded to descend the steps, her black boots, incongruous in the heat, clanging on the metal steps. With each step she considered his words. *Claimed.* It should have appalled her but instead the possessive word sent a delicious shivering of sensation skittering through her body, nestling somewhere deep and private inside of her.

She felt almost shy when she looked up at him when he joined her on the tarmac. He offered her his arm.

She owed him, she reminded herself firmly as she slipped her hand through his arm. But it hardly felt like a penance—the smooth silk of his jacket under her hand, the heat rising up from his skin, a reminder of when he picked her up and held her close—no, not a penance, more like a reward. "I hope." She cleared her throat, trying not to dwell on her increased heartbeat and the distracting tingling sensations that coursed through her body, when he touched his hand over hers. "I hope," she repeated, "there's no-one around to witness this. One, I don't want your fiancée to get the wrong idea. And two, I think I'm going to look pretty odd on the arm of a Prince, dressed like a Prince, while I'm most definitely dressed like someone who's just walked in from the farm."

"I doubt there'll be any paparazzi here. They weren't expecting me."

"Paparazzi?" She hadn't even thought of them.

"Yes. They're tiresome, but not as intrusive as in Europe. We usually allow them a few photos and that satisfies the newspapers." Suddenly there was a flash. "Spoke too soon," Sahmir said grimly. Whoever had taken the photograph must have quickly disappeared because there was no sign of anyone other than airport security as they moved through the marble foyer.

They were met at the entrance to the airport building by two men who escorted them through the formalities. They were soon in a sleek air-conditioned black limo, driving along a magnificent street lined with palm trees and designer shops. Western clothes and middle eastern robes blended into a cosmopolitan mix.

She cast a quick glance at Sahmir. He looked more Parisian than Middle Eastern. "Do you normally wear robes?"

"For formal occasions at the palace, yes. My brother, the King, wears them more often. But I'm only the tolerated youngest brother, who's more often overseas than in Ma'in. I have a knack for making money, Rory, not only through gambling. So I spend a lot of time in Europe and in the States. And most people expect to see me in the best Italian suits. I try not to disappoint."

"I guess no-one will mind me wearing my old clothes?" She plucked at her jeans, hardly believing that she was concerned at such a thing. But she felt so out of place.

"Yes, they will. That's why I've instructed that there be clothes waiting for you."

"But I don't have the money for clothes! I can't repay you."

He sighed. "Rory, you seem to forget that I am extremely wealthy and that I can easily afford a few items of clothing for you. Besides"—he cocked an amused eyebrow—"I've only seen you either in an indecent evening dress or equally indecent jeans and t-shirt. Which, to be honest, I'm not complaining about. But I thought you might like a change."

She pulled her sweater closer around her chest. "The evening dress was a vintage piece of my mother's I picked out from her wardrobe at the last minute. I thought it might prove useful. I don't possess any other posh clothes. There's always something to be done on my estate."

"Not *your* estate any more, I'm afraid."

"I know. I just can't believe it. I loved that place. It was old, falling apart, but the land was good. I could have made something of it. I know I could. I had plans…"

"What plans?"

"Farming. I grew up with the land and knew what it could do. I studied it at university. I could have made it wealthy again."

"You studied agricultural science?"

"Yes. I have a degree in it. It was the only thing I wanted to do. Maman tried to get me to study Art History. But I couldn't tell a van Gogh from a van Morrison."

He raised an eyebrow. "Van Morrison? He's a singer."

She sighed. "You see? There was no point in trying to make me into a lady. I was a tomboy growing up and a tomboy I've stayed."

"Hmm… I probably should have discovered this fact before I ordered you some clothes."

"I'm sure," she said trying to repress the image of a wardrobe of flowery, feminine dresses which she'd normally never agree to wear. She owed him. "I'm sure they'll be fine. I'm very grateful. Thank you."

Sahmir's smile suggested he saw right through her words. "You're most welcome." He glanced out the window. "We're here."

CLAIMED BY THE SHEIKH

Rory followed his gaze to a wide sweep of stairs, bright white, even under the sheltering portico. A liveried footman opened the door for her. Sahmir joined her and they walked up the front steps and into the most amazing space she'd ever seen. She was suddenly aware of the immense wealth of the country, and of Sahmir, who looked totally at home in the opulent surroundings.

"This way," he said smoothly, as they walked straight ahead, through the impressive entrance hall. She noticed he glanced up at a wall of floor to ceiling opaque windows, urging her on a little faster through the public space.

One room unfolded into another until at last they came to a set of stairs that had a more domestic look about it. "This is my wing of the palace." He opened the first door and she entered the room. It was a beautiful bedroom. Through an open door she could see a dressing room. Plus doors which presumably led to a bathroom. "I hope this is all right for you?"

"Are you kidding? It's more than all right. It's beautiful." And it was. From the apricot velvet drapes, to the plush cream carpet, it was delicious and she couldn't resist brushing her hands over the drapes as she opened the window and leaned out. She gasped. "The garden!" They were one floor above ground level but the trees grew higher than them, and the climbing plants clung to the palace walls, allowing their blooms to scent the air directly outside the window.

"You like it?"

She turned, surprised to hear his voice suddenly so close by. "It's amazing. What are those flowers, there?" She reached out to an extravagant bloom but couldn't touch it. So she jumped and pushed herself up, her jersey slipping as she did so, and falling to the floor, until her hips were supported on the wide sill and she stretched to touch the blossom, clutching the sill quickly with both hands as she slipped a little.

"Be careful!" His hands were around her hips, keeping her secure and for a brief moment she felt his body pressed up behind hers. She cried out in surprise and he stepped back. "I'm sorry. I thought you were going to fall."

"No. I've climbed huge trees on the estate and not fallen. I've a good head for heights. Came in pretty useful getting away last night." She frowned. "What would you have done if there was no drainpipe?"

"No idea. We'd have had a longer jump I guess. Just as well Farouq is a good catch and is as strong as a horse." He paused and she wondered why he was grinning. He indicated her shirt and she looked down. "*Merde!*" She clamped her hands over her chest. Not only was the shape of her breasts clearly visible, the bra revealed her nipples all too clearly. It looked as if she wasn't wearing anything.

"Just as well you kept your jersey over you earlier." He backed away and she frowned. "I'll leave you to it. I'd best go and find my brother. I'll see you later." He turned and walked away quickly.

She didn't understand his expression, one that was both concentrated and frowning, as if not understanding something. Nor did she understand his abrupt exit. Had he been angry about something?

SAHMIR STOOD at the top of the stairs for a few moments, waiting for his body to return to normal. He gripped the banisters and gazed unseeing at the marble floor at the bottom. All he could think of was the shape of her breasts and the effect they had on his body. For a brief moment he imagined how they would feel in his hands, how they would taste... And of her body's response to his ministrations.

It did nothing to make his arousal disappear. Instead he thought of his brother's disapproval, of his country's need of him and, not least, his sister who'd always wanted him to do the right thing. He sighed. His sister had always been fighting a losing battle—first with him, and then with her life.

It was all he needed to enable him to walk quickly down the stairs and back through the public areas. He saw Tariq's assistant, Aarif, emerging from one of the rooms.

"Where's the King?"

Aarif looked uncharacteristically harried. "I'm trying to find him. He seems to have disappeared."

Sahmir frowned. "That's not like him. Can you send for me when you find him? I'll go and say hello to the kids."

Sahmir walked through to Tariq's family quarters and was greeted by the children.

Within half an hour, he'd caught up with the latest boy band that Saarah was a fan of, the pet that Gadiel had adopted, much to his sister's disgust, and the new words the youngest one, Eshal, was speaking. But even more interesting than that, he'd been told of a woman, called Cara, who Tariq had introduced them to.

Gadiel had just finished describing in gory detail how he fed locusts to his pet and had decided to argue with his sister about something, when Sahmir turned around and saw a woman, short and slim, hesitating on the threshold, a look of shock on her face as he caught her eye.

He walked out of the room toward her. "Are you okay?"

"Sure. Sorry, I just wasn't expecting anyone other than the children."

"Nor was I." Her voice! The voice from a chocolate advertisement. So the plan he'd hatched before he'd left to get his brother together with the woman with the sexy voice, had worked, better than he could have hoped. He grinned and extended his hand to hers. "I'm Sahmir, Tariq's youngest brother, and you must be the Cara I've heard so much about."

"Yes." She shook his hand. "Tariq said you were in Paris."

"Yes. I'm back earlier than anticipated."

"Did you have a good trip?"

He grimaced. "Shall we say 'interesting'? Care for a drink?"

"Please. A coffee would be great."

He poured two coffees and returned to the table.

"Uncle Sahmir! Come back and play." Gadiel's voice drifted out the door.

"Later!"

"Please, don't let me stop you from playing with your nieces and nephew."

"I'll play with them later. Besides, I don't often get a chance to talk to a woman Tariq has introduced to his children."

Cara lowered her eyes and took a sip of the hot, black coffee. She looked tired. No doubt his rigid brother hadn't made life easy for her.

"I believe you employed me, Your Royal Highness."

"Please, call me Sahmir. And yes, I did employ you. I have to admit, I fell for your voice on the chocolate ad. And…"

"And you imagined me to be a femme fatale who would amuse your brother for a few weeks. Give him some light relief from his work." She took another sip, and Sahmir was relieved to see humor in her narrowed eyes.

"Um, looks like you can see right through me. But I have to say"—he grinned—"my plan seems to have worked."

She suddenly looked uncomfortable. "I'm leaving in a few hours."

"Ah, so maybe it didn't work as well as I'd imagined. Shame. So… where are you headed?"

"England."

"For a holiday?"

"Just a week or so to tie up some loose ends and then I'm moving to Italy."

He sighed. "That really *is* a shame."

She shrugged awkwardly. "No, it's not. There's nothing to keep me here."

He rose. "Not even Tariq?"

She rose too. "Especially not Tariq."

Just at that moment the children noticed her through the open double doors. "Cara!"

Sahmir gave a low whistle and looked from Cara back to the children. "On first name terms with Tariq's children?" He watched with interest as Eshal toddled up to Cara, attached herself to her leg and Cara petted her head. "On more than first name terms with Eshal!" He laughed and gathered the girl in his arms, twisting her around until she was shrieking with laughter.

When Sahmir had successfully diverted the children, he turned once more to Cara. He was dying to know what was going on.

"So have you seen Tariq in the last hour?" Cara asked. "Is... is he okay?"

"Not that I want to pry"—he shrugged—"although I probably do, but why do you think Tariq wouldn't be okay?"

"Just wondered."

"All right. You're as discreet as Tariq, I get it. Even if you do give more away in your eyes than he does. Anyway, I don't know how he is. I haven't seen him yet. I'm putting off the evil moment when I introduce him to a... a lady who's with me."

"Your fiancée? Tariq told me you were getting engaged."

"*He* told you that?"

"Sorry, I didn't think. No doubt it's private, family stuff. He only mentioned it in passing."

"That's okay. It's just that Tariq rarely talks about family matters to anyone outside the family. He must have trusted you."

She shrugged. "So where is she? Your fiancée?"

"She's not my fiancée. She's freshening up. She's had a hell of a time and she's resting before it's topped off by my brother's displeasure."

Cara frowned. "Why would Tariq be displeased with meeting your fiancée-to-be? He was expecting her."

"The lady who's with me isn't the woman I'm going to marry."

"Oh! And Tariq doesn't know yet?"

"No, not yet. He seems to have disappeared without trace. Even Aarif doesn't know where he is." He raised an eyebrow. "Have you any idea?"

She shook her head.

"Any clue as to his mood?"

She grimaced. "Not a good one, I'm afraid."

"Oh. You, too?"

She nodded. "It was my fault. I neglected to tell him something important."

"Couldn't have been that important."

"Oh, yes, it was."

"You can tell me, you know. I'm the extrovert brother; Tariq's the introvert and Daidan, the middle brother, well, only Allah knows what Daidan is."

"He's in Finland, I understand?"

"Yes. In the cold snowy north, mining diamonds. He's even worse than Tariq when it comes to emotional stuff." He leaned forward. "So tell me what it was you should have told him. Maybe I can help."

"Thank you, but nothing can help. I'm married, you see. To a man who doesn't love me, and whom I don't love. We've not been 'together' for years now. And I haven't known where he was for some of that time so I haven't been able to get a divorce."

"And you told Tariq that?"

"Sort of, but he wouldn't listen."

"Of course he wouldn't." Damn Tariq and his rigid moral code. It was stopping him from seeing what was right before his eyes. This girl was perfect for him. He needed to be told. "Look, I have to go and sort a few things out. Hope to see you later." He rose and kissed her hand. "Lovely to meet you, Cara. I hope we meet again."

He didn't wait for her reply, so anxious was he to find Tariq. To tell him that Tariq shouldn't let a small thing like the woman he cared about being married get in the way. These things could be sorted out. And that his youngest brother had brought home a woman who wasn't the woman he was destined to marry. He sighed. Life could be so complicated sometimes.

Sahmir was about to knock on Tariq's door but Tariq opened it suddenly, with a face like thunder. He waved a newspaper at him. "What the hell have you been up to?"

"And hello to you, dear brother. Thank you for the welcome." He walked over to the dresser and poured himself a coffee. "Like one?"

"No. What I'd like is to know what's going on. Here." He dropped the paper onto the table in front of Sahmir.

Sahmir didn't pick it up immediately but drank some of his coffee. He needed caffeine before he could take on his brother.

"'Lady of the night' and 'gutters of Paris' would be bad enough, but you're *together*?'"

The Russian. Sahmir should have realized he'd not heard the last. "She's not a lady of the night," he said smoothly.

"You know," Tariq continued as if Sahmir hadn't spoken, "I'd have thought it was the usual tabloid lies, if it hadn't been for the photograph. *You*. Ma'in airport. And this... this *woman*."

Sahmir frowned, unfolded the newspaper and looked at the front page of the evening news. He and Rory featured, emerging from the plane. The wind from the engines must have caught her hair because it was tousled and her eyes were narrowed sexily, no doubt because of the bright sunshine. But she looked for all the world like she'd just had sex. Rough sex. The red bruise on her cheekbone was prominent in the photo.

The Russian was determined to drag Rory down. And him. He sat down and tossed away the paper.

"Guilty, as snapped." He sighed. "Unfortunate."

"What the hell is Safiyeh and her family going to think?"

"That I haven't changed much, I should imagine. Little else." He shrugged. "We both know why we're getting married—for the convenience and future of both our countries."

"I hope you're right."

Tariq picked up the paper and read out loud the caption beneath the photo.

"Who's the mysterious brunette wearing worn-out clothes and a black eye, accompanying Prince Sahmir?"

"We have it on high authority that she's a 'lady of the night' picked up by Prince Sahmir from the gutters of Paris.

Unfortunately our source wouldn't divulge how the brunette came by the black eye. Could she have received it from the Prince himself?"

"Who the hell is she, Sahmir? Even *if* Safiyeh accepts the situation, what is her family going to say when they see you spread across the cover of the paper with this cheap—"

"Stop right there, Tariq." Sahmir was rarely angry but the

injustice was too much to bear. He could hardly think straight as he rose from his seat and stood, too close to Tariq. "You can say what the hell you like about me. But not Rory."

"Rory?"

"Aurora. Known to her friends as Rory."

"And you, I take it, are one of her friends?"

"Yes."

Sahmir was so close he could see a muscle clench in Tariq's jaw as he tried to contain his anger. Tariq's eyes were like fire. He curled his lip with disdain. "Why did you take up with her, jeopardizing your marriage to Safiyeh, and all that entails… the lands… the wealth and power?"

"It won't jeopardize anything. Safiyeh and her family are realists. They want what marriage to me will bring politically. That's all. Nothing's changed."

Tariq's eyes narrowed. He looked away, hesitated and then walked over to the sideboard and poured himself a coffee. He indicated to Sahmir that he should sit down and he came and sat opposite. He sighed. "Do you remember when we were boys? You came out to Qusayr Zarqa and you found a wounded bird in the wadi under the wild pistachio trees?"

Sahmir frowned. "Of course I remember. What's that to do with anything?"

Tariq held Sahmir's gaze as he sipped his hot coffee. "I can remember Mama's scream when she discovered it nestled in a drawer in your room, complete with the splint you'd made for it and the worms in case it became hungry."

Sahmir grunted. "It got well though, didn't it?"

"It did. You cried for days after it flew away."

"Cried? Me?"

"I heard you, in your room when you thought no-one could hear you."

"But you didn't come to me?"

"Of course not. That wasn't how we were brought up, was it? And nor was being kind to waifs and strays. Seems you haven't changed much."

Sahmir rubbed his eyes that stung from lack of sleep. "I had no choice, Tariq. She was in the wrong place at the wrong time with the wrong people. I had to get her out of there."

"What's she like?"

"She's…" He couldn't think how to describe her. 'She's nice' wouldn't do it. Stick to the facts. "She's from Roche. It's a tiny principality in the south of France. She's an aristocrat with no money and no estate, a tomboy, a lover of nature and the land. She's so far from being a cheap whore, it's not funny."

"And you like her."

"I like her, but I hardly know her."

"How long is she going to stay here?"

"Until it's safe for her to leave."

"You don't want her to go, do you? Just like the bird whose wing you mended all those years ago. You want to hold on to her."

Sahmir nudged the coffee cup further onto the table, for something to do, something to hide the fact that, yes, he liked her very much. He shrugged in what he hoped was a nonchalant fashion. "Yes, I do."

"Then I'm sorry."

Sahmir rubbed his mouth uncertainly then looked up at Tariq. "We don't need this marriage any more, do we? Not after what we both pulled off with the gold mine. Ma'in is set now for many years to come. It's safe."

"It'll be safer with the might of Safiyeh's country behind us. Besides, *we* can't break it off. It's not honorable and we don't want to make an enemy out of our neighbors."

Sahmir looked down and shook his head. "No. I

guess not."

"Any suggestion that the marriage wouldn't go ahead would have to come from them. And Safiyeh's father isn't likely to change his mind. Even with this scandal. So, Rory. You know you can't be together here in Ma'in? You do realize that we have to go into damage control, that we have to bring the engagement forward? I've spoken with the King and he agrees. Safiyeh will arrive in a few days to show to the public that the engagement will still go ahead. Except sooner than anyone imagined," he added grimly.

Sahmir slowly nodded. "Rory can stay at Qusayr Zarqa. I'll take her there. I'll not leave her immediately," he added stubbornly. "I'll have a few days in her company and then we'll part. Then"—he turned to Tariq—"I promise to focus on the business to hand."

"And you'll return and stay here, in the city." Tariq nodded. "It could work. Now all you have to do is charm both women into going along with this plan. It can't be hard —someone with your skills in that department."

Sahmir smiled. "Thank you for your faith in my charm, Tariq. It may come as news to you that not every woman loves me."

"Of course they do. Unlike me, you have an unerring way with women."

Sahmir remembered his exchange with Cara. "Unlike you? That's not what I've been hearing."

Tariq's face suddenly looked dangerous. "And what have you been hearing?"

"I bumped into a friend of yours when I looked in on the kids. Lovely lady. We had a nice long chat."

"About what?"

"She told me she neglected to tell you something important."

"You *did* have a heart-to-heart."

"She's married to a man she doesn't love and a divorce is imminent."

"She told you that?"

"She did. And apparently you were too full of righteous indignation and moral superiority to listen to her."

"She told you that, also?"

"No, I imagined that. But I'm sure I'm right. I *know* you, Tariq. And Cara is fantastic. She's seems exactly the right woman for you. She can't help being married. Sounds like a divorce is imminent anyway. She probably didn't tell you because it was none of your business initially. She was working for you, that was all. But"—he grinned—"obviously the relationship changed and no doubt by that time, she couldn't find the right moment to tell you. Forget it. You know now. Don't throw away a chance at happiness just because she's married.

Tariq sat back heavily in his chair. "I know. You're right. I was about to go to see her. Is she still with the children?"

"She is."

Tariq jumped up and walked decisively over to the door. There he turned. "I'll see you later." He smiled, a rare smile. "It's good to have you back, Sahmir."

He walked over and gave Tariq a hug. "It's good to be home."

After Tariq left, Sahmir sat down at the desk and picked up the newspaper once more. There was the photograph of the two of them descending the steps at the airport. There was no doubt about it. Rory looked as beautiful and as sexy as hell, despite the bruised cheek. His body responded on cue.

Damn. Because of that photo he was being thrust into a marriage he didn't want, sooner than was necessary. But he still had two days in which to enjoy Rory's company. He'd just better make them good ones.

CHAPTER 5

Another day, another photo. Sahmir tossed the morning paper onto his desk and sighed.

There was no doubt about it. Aurora de Chambéry was infinitely photogenic. Whether she was looking indecently sexual as in the photograph from the evening paper the previous day, or like this, supremely elegant as she stepped out of the palace to investigate the gardens, her face in profile, her bruised cheek hidden, as she gazed across the gardens, thoughtful and poignant. While he? He was staring at her from the doorway like a hungry predator. He closed the newspaper with a snap.

He jumped up and took his coffee to a window, looking out onto the city that sparkled in the early morning light.

Somewhere out there the Russian had people watching his, and Rory's, every move. The thought made his skin crawl.

Was it a warning that he'd come for her? That he'd really killed someone and believed Rory had witnessed it?

Or was it simply a reminder to Sahmir that the Russian wasn't happy and that he was watching them—a smear campaign to ruin their reputations? And it was working. Sahmir knew, more than anyone, the power of the media.

Years before, his messy attempts to reconcile with a woman he'd loved, after she'd left him to return to her domineering and abusive father, had been splattered all over the papers. He'd retreated into a dark world from which he'd only been rescued by the love of his sister. But he'd emerged tougher and he'd never make either mistake again—not let someone, or something, take control of him.

Whatever the Russian's motives, he had to get Rory away for a while, away from prying eyes, away from the interest of the public. And away from him. And there was only one place that would do that.

SAHMIR HESITATED outside the connecting door, listening for any sign of movement. There was none. He knocked gently. There was a muffled sound and then... nothing. He placed his hand on the handle, gripped it and was about to depress it, but withdrew it instead. Rory didn't even know his room was connected to hers. It was too soon to walk in on her without warning.

Just as he was about to walk away, the door opened and she stood there, still dressed in jeans and that incredible t-shirt. He lifted his gaze. "How are you?"

She backed away and folded her arms over her chest after seeing the direction of his glance. She nodded. "Fine."

"May I come in?"

She shrugged. "Why not? My room looks to be a part of your bedroom suite, anyway."

"It is. But I'll always knock first. If you don't want me to come in, don't answer. I won't insist on entry, Rory. You don't know me well, but I'd have thought you'd have understood *that* at least about me by now."

She smiled briefly. "Yes. I guess I do." She opened the door wide. "You can come in, if you like."

"Thank you." He followed her in and looked around and stood, his hands in the pockets of his trousers, feeling ill at ease in his own suite. Then he returned his gaze to Rory who had returned to the window seat where she'd obviously been sitting before he'd come in.

He'd brought women back to the palace before and they'd always been delighted, flitting around, checking out the luxurious bathroom, the elegant suite. But Rory? She'd only left the suite to walk in the gardens and then had retired to bed for the night. No doubt she was traumatized by what had happened to her. But how could he help if she wouldn't talk to him?

"You haven't changed. Did you sleep in these clothes? Weren't the clothes I bought to your liking?" He walked over to the wardrobe for something to do and opened it. He ran his hand over the racks of clothes—formal, casual and everything in between. "There must be something here to your taste. I had the store pick one of just about everything." He turned back to her. She was studying him carefully. "I wasn't sure what you'd like."

"They're all beautiful."

"I sense a 'but'."

"But... they're not mine. I didn't buy them. I feel uncomfortable keeping on taking from you. And I don't understand why you're going out of your way to help me."

Nor did he. He selected some wide-legged white linen trousers and a beautifully cut silk shirt. "Here, why not change into these. That's about as tomboyish as there is."

"You've not answered my question."

He looked up innocently. "I didn't realize you'd asked me one."

"Why are you helping me?"

Why indeed? He sighed. "What would you have me do? Hide you away in a corner of the palace dressed in that indecent t-shirt and jeans?"

She crossed her arms over her t-shirt. "You can if you like."

"I *don't* like. Now, come on. You left the suite only once yesterday with me to check out the garden. I've given you some space but now it's time to move. I thought I'd show you a little more of our country."

She sighed and shook her head, the brittle, defensive attitude disappearing immediately. "I'm sorry, Sahmir. You've been so kind and I don't want to be a burden to you. Why not just leave me here alone and you can go about your business."

"You want to sit out the month, here, in your bedroom? That's fine. I'll return in a month to blow the cobwebs off you, and return you to Europe, a lot leaner than when you arrived."

He got the smile he was after.

"But, in a way, you're correct. I can't spend all my time with you. It'll jeopardize my brother's—I mean *our*—plans. We've decided it'll be best if you stay at our hunting lodge, away from the prying eyes of the paparazzi and my future in-laws."

"Hunting lodge? What's it like?"

"I'll take you there later today. If it's not to your liking, we'll find somewhere else. But unfortunately, after tomorrow, it'll have to be away from me." He smiled, encouragingly. "Come on, I'm not going to suggest you spend your time in some hole of a place, am I? It's not such a bad suggestion. You can see something of my country, taste some of the wonderful food we have here."

She rose. "You're right. I'm being stupid. I just feel a bit shell-shocked. I'm sorry. I'll do whatever you suggest. I spoke

CLAIMED BY THE SHEIKH

to Maman this morning and she's so grateful for all you've done to find them a place in St Malo."

"My pleasure. And it'll also be my pleasure to see you change into these clothes, pack a bag for a couple of nights, and we'll go into the desert and I'll show you Qusayr Zarqa."

"The hunting lodge?" She smiled. "I imagine a remote wooden lodge complete with deer heads on the walls."

Sahmir grinned. "Um, not so much like that. But it *is* remote which will be good."

She frowned suspiciously. "Why?"

He indicated the paper on the table. "To get away from this."

She picked up the paper and read. He watched her skin pale. She dropped it back onto the table. "He's never going to leave us—me—alone, is he?"

"No, not until we've sorted out the estate. I've spoken with my lawyers and they seem quite confident something can be done. I've instructed them to keep working on the case until it's resolved. Rest assured, Rory, we won't leave any stone unturned. Now, let's talk of more pleasant things. Can you ride?"

Her face lit up. "We're going horse riding? Sahmir! I love horses. Where? When?"

"Tomorrow, at Qusayr Zarqa. After you've met the rest of the family. And... if you're still feeling you owe me, there *is* a way you can repay me."

Suspicion immediately clouded her features. "How?"

"You can enjoy yourself. Give me the pleasure of watching you relax. Okay?"

She smiled. "I'm sorry. Of course." She picked the clothes up from the bed. "I'll get changed."

"Good. And then I'll show you around the palace and you can meet my brother and my nieces and nephew. And my cousins—they're twins—are arriving this afternoon too, back from England to stay. Then we'll travel into the desert. Show you something of our heritage, check out our horses."

She smiled. But it didn't reach her eyes. She was just being brave. But that was good enough for him... for now.

~

THE AFTERNOON HAD BEEN MORE enjoyable than Rory had imagined. She spent it with the King's family, introduced simply as a friend who was passing through.

She'd watched Sahmir as he played cricket with his nephew. Sahmir looked like a big kid. His hair was longer than his brother's—whom she'd briefly met and less briefly been scared of—and, with his shirt-sleeves pushed up and his face concentrating as he delivered a spin ball to his nephew, he could have been at an English public school. Playful, handsome and definitely charming. Then he looked up at her and her heart gave a sudden patter and she found herself blushing. She looked away. She never blushed.

"Rory." He said her name softly, with that wonderful accent of his and she turned to look up at him. "It's time to leave. Shall we go?" He held out his hand to her.

Four hours ago, she'd have backed away like a wounded dog, afraid of a kicking. But now she reached out and took his hand and he pulled her up to standing.

"Ah, to this mysterious hunting lodge."

"Not so very mysterious."

She was tall but still a head shorter than him. He was breathing quickly from his exertions at cricket and his breath was warm on her face. Without thinking she licked her lips and glanced down at his lips. He'd done the same thing. Then his lips quirked into a smile as he placed her hand on his arm. "We'll go the long way around and walk through the gardens, if you like?"

She grinned. "I like."

It was late afternoon and the sun was too low to penetrate the courtyard gardens. Instead the light had an almost romantic quality about it—soft and dewy under the watering the gardeners had just given it.

Although there were palace buildings on all sides, the gardens were enormous and they were soon lost amidst towering plants and fragrant flowers. She sighed, utterly seduced by the beauty of the rampant nature all around her. "This is gorgeous." She trailed her free hand along freshly watered flowers, the disturbed plants issuing a beautiful fragrance up into the evening air. "This is so different to Senlisse."

"Tell me about Senlisse."

She sighed again, a sigh edged in nostalgia. "This time of year? It'd either be buried under snow—the estate isn't far from the Alps—with the chestnut trees in the woods stark against the snow and iron-grey sky. Black rooks would be cawing and circling around The Mount. That's where the original castle was."

"The land has been owned by your family since then?"

"Longer than that. For over nine hundred years it's been owned and lived in by the de Chambéry family." She was silent as she rubbed the water from the flowers between her fingers and felt the hurt of losing the estate, anew. "But not any more." She looked up to his interested face with a lighthearted smile she didn't feel. "Now it's the property of the Russian mafia, who won't know which trees can be felled or which fields need tending to—" She broke off abruptly, unsure if her voice would hold steady.

He stopped walking and she stopped too, trying desperately to hold it together. "If life has taught me anything, it's that you can never know what's ahead of you. A week ago, who'd have thought I'd be walking through these gardens with a beautiful French tomboy."

"Not French. Roche is a separate country, with separate laws," she breathed.

"Same language, though. Same French words coming from those beautiful lips of yours."

With one smooth movement he dipped his head and brushed his lips against hers. Before she could register what he'd done, he'd pulled back and looked away, as if he, too, couldn't believe it. Nor could she. And yet it felt entirely natural.

They were back walking along the path before she knew it. She touched her lips with her hand and wondered if she'd imagined it. But then she caught his gaze and saw the same heat she could feel within her. She hadn't imagined the kiss and she hadn't imagined her response to it, or his. And more shockingly, it hadn't scared her. It had left her wanting more. And that most definitely *did* scare her. She withdrew her hand from his and looked straight ahead.

"Have..."

"Yes?"

She drew in a deep breath. "Have you always lived here?"

"Ah…" He realized she was changing the subject, pushing distance between them again. "Yes, I have. Tariq spent most of his youth in the desert with our grandparents. I grew up here with my parents."

"Just you?"

"No. I had an elder sister, Ensiyeh, and Daidan, who lives in Finland. They all stayed here in the city. Tariq and my father didn't see eye to eye so grandfather kept Tariq with him, probably for his own safety. My father had a temper."

"And where's your sister?"

Rory counted six paces as they walked in silence, waiting for him to answer. But he didn't immediately. Then he stopped and plucked a flower, smelled it and passed it to her. "This was my sister's favorite flower. She used to say that it was so beautiful it had no need of perfume."

Rory brought it to her nose and smelled it. Sure enough, there was no fragrance. She touched the velvet white petals and the brightly colored pattern that emerged like a butterfly from its center. "No doubt this did the job of attracting the bees sufficiently to pollinate."

He gave a brief laugh. "So answers the farmer." They continued walking. "Ensiyeh wasn't a farmer. She was a philosopher. She was wise, too wise for this world."

"What happened?"

"When influenza came to our city, I did what I'd been forbidden to do and went to play with my friends in the city. I contracted it, spent weeks scaring my family half to death before recovering completely."

"You were lucky."

"Yes. But my sister was not. She'd never been strong and she caught it from me and afterwards contracted rheumatic fever. Her heart was affected. She was an invalid for years and died of it a few years ago. I've never forgiven myself."

"But you couldn't help it."

"Yes, I could. I should have done as my parents told me, and stayed away from my friends."

"You were young. There's no way you should blame yourself."

"Sometimes it's easy to think one thing but to feel another. I doubt that feeling will ever release its grip." He sighed, long and hard, his eyes narrowed. "You know, I miss my sister, every day."

A lump rose in Rory's throat. His words were so simple but they moved her. As he spoke them, she'd seen behind that charming, easy smile, behind that superficial smoothness that was so disarming, to a raw pain that was always there, nagging and hurting him, driving his every action.

He cleared his throat and glanced at her. "Anyway, that's enough of me. Let's get going. Dinner awaits at Qusayr Zarqa. I'll be interested to see what you think of the place."

"I'm sure I'll like it. And I love horses." She was pretty sure she'd like anything that Sahmir suggested right that moment. Revealing the pain of the loss of his sister had done more to reassure her that she was safe with him than anything else could have done.

They climbed the steps to their suite. He left her at her door and went down the corridor to his separate entrance. She hesitated at the door, watching him walk down the marble hallway—pristine and immaculate, the late sun shining in through the high clerestory windows. It cast a spotlight over him as if he were a star walking along a stage. His longish hair curled carelessly around his collar and his broad shoulders, the perfect frame for his white shirt, half untucked by his recent exertions at cricket. Again, she felt desire for him stir within her. This time it was heightened, unleashed by the revelation that this God among men was a fallible God, a hurt God.

CHAPTER 6

The sun had dipped behind the horizon by the time they reached Qusayr Zarqa. Rory's spirits had fallen with each mile they moved from the city, with its hidden, well-tended oases and green strip of mangroves that edged the ocean. The landscape became more and more alien —raw, empty of green, empty of life, it seemed to her. It was a different world to the one she'd left behind in France.

"Qusayr Zarqa," Sahmir indicated. "Up ahead."

She squinted into the light that was bright despite her sunglasses. "It's a rock."

"It *was* a rock, a couple of thousand years ago. For the last thousand years at least it's been a castle."

"Your hunting lodge is a castle?" She smiled to herself. Her image of a log cabin, albeit on a grand and luxurious scale, evaporated. "So what do you do out here, in a thousand-year-old castle?"

"It has up-to-date technology thanks to the security we had installed when we moved some of our ancient Ma'inese artefacts here. Before that, we'd sometimes turn off the electricity and enjoy the castle as it must have been in medieval times. Tariq used to do it all the time—it drove the kitchen staff mad."

"And the horses?" she asked hopefully.

"Lots of horses. They were a passion of my mother's. She kept them at Qusayr Zarqa and retreated here when life with my father got too difficult. It gave her time to catch up with Tariq, too. He spent a lot of time here, growing up with my grandparents."

"Sounds complicated. Obviously some things, like families, don't change—royal or not."

"Yes, relationships aren't something which my family has been a complete success with."

"And you're continuing the family tradition. Bringing home one woman, when you're about to become engaged to another."

Putting the facts so baldly had them both in silence as they turned off the main highway and onto a smaller road that led straight up to the castle.

For all her earlier dismissal of the castle, Rory had to admit it was amazing. She'd never seen architecture like it. It emerged from the surrounding desert, the same color and texture, but its square, uncompromising design was all about asserting the ancient desert sheikhs' authority over their people.

Its front entrance was framed with a three story high arch, and along the top the facade was pierced with square windows. Turrets protruded at each side of the facade.

"Your ancestors must have been building your estate around the same time as mine were building this," Sahmir commented.

"It's that old?"

He pulled up the car in front of the entrance and turned off the engine. "Eighth century, so the experts tell us."

She whistled low. "It wasn't until a couple of centuries after that, that my ancestors built the first castle at Senlisse. Pretty basic compared to this."

"At the time this was built, my ancestors had conquered vast lands. The history is recorded on the frescoes inside. It was built as both a fortress and a pleasure palace." He grinned. "My people knew how to enjoy themselves."

"Out here? In the middle of nowhere?"

"Nowhere?" he repeated softly, his criticism implicit. "It's only 'nowhere' to strangers. To people who don't understand."

"You're right. But I'm still a stranger, Sahmir. It still feels like nowhere to me."

"Of course. But, to my ancestors, it was the center of their world, the center of civilization." He opened the door. "Come on, I'll show you round."

Before she'd finished collecting her things, Sahmir had opened her door for her. She jumped out of the air-conditioned car into the heat of the desert, a little less intense now it was nearing evening.

What struck her as they walked up to the castle was that there was no impressive sweep of steps, no ornate portico to disguise the fact that this was very much a fortress. Instead, huge wooden doors swung open and men emerged in traditional robes and greeted them. Sahmir stopped and spoke to them in Arabic and then they melted away, leaving just the two of them in the vast hallway.

She turned full circle, looking up at the paintings that covered the walls and the vaulted ceiling. "This is amazing!"

"Yes, on all my travels, I've never seen anything come close to this." He pointed to one wall, on which a number of men were depicted. "That's the fresco which shows the extent of the Caliph's empire at that time. He's shown at the center, along with the kings he's vanquished. They include the Byzantine emperor, as well as the Visigothic king of Spain. And others. And over there"—he turned and pointed to the far side of the hall—"lies the bath complex. The *hammam*. Would you like to see it now? Or maybe you'd like to rest before dinner? What would you like to do?"

It was all so alien to her, so imposing, so different, she felt a need to see something familiar. "I'd love to see the horses."

He laughed. "It wasn't what I imagined you say, but that's fine. They're round the back."

As they walked over to the stables, which were hidden from public view in the compound that extended behind the castle, Sahmir reflected that this was *not* how he imagined spending the first evening with Rory at Qusayr Zarqa.

He'd pictured them sitting on the terrace, drinking champagne, maybe even flirting a little. Only a little, he reassured his conscience. Instead, as they entered the stables, he was inhaling the pungent smell of horse dung.

But there were compensations. With her attention solely taken up with the horses, he was free to drink in his fill of her. Even in the plainest pants and shirt, she looked amazing. With her olive skin and long dark hair she could have been from a neighboring land where the skin was lighter and the eyes often blue. She might feel a stranger, but she looked totally at home here.

As she walked through the stables, stopping to pet and talk to the different horses, she asked questions he had to refer to the stable-hand. He had no idea and no interest. But Rory's interest in horses most definitely wasn't feigned.

"When can we go riding?"

"Tomorrow. There's not enough daylight left to travel to where I have in mind."

"Where's that?" She patted a horse and went onto the next one. The horse's eyes followed her longingly and Sahmir knew how he felt.

"Jabal al Noor—the gold mine that's now been handed back to us. Now that the Aurus Group have left, Tariq's given orders for it to be dismantled."

"Aren't you going to continue to mine the gold?"

"No. There *is* gold left, but the place is a mess. We have other plans. The river had been diverted by Aurus but we'll revert it back to its original course and drown the whole thing. Create a reservoir from which local farmers can irrigate the land. It'll transform the land."

"Wow. That sounds interesting, *and* a challenge. What kind of crops are you going to grow?"

Sahmir shrugged and walked on to the open door at the end of the stables and looked out. "I'm not sure. I've left the detail up to Tariq. No doubt he has something planned."

"I'll be interested to hear because I did my thesis on farming marginal land. There's research going on at the moment about switching from food crops to relatively unknown biofuel crops." She glanced at him. "Not the usual biofuel crops, because they're proving unsustainable."

"Oh." It was all he could say. He knew nothing about either usual, or unusual, biofuel crops. "You should talk to Tariq about it. I'm sure he'd be interested."

"And that means you're not?"

"I'm interested that you're interested. Put it like that."

Sahmir leaned against the doorjamb, looking out at the line of wild pistachio trees that signaled the entrance to the wadi, which wound its way up along the valley floor and eventually into the hills. He returned his gaze to Rory.

The afternoon sun was low and filtered through the trees onto her. She stood nuzzling a white mare, talking softly to it while the horse breathed noisily as if answering her. Rory's dark hair fell over her face and around her shoulders, its red highlights gleaming in the light.

When had it happened, he thought to himself? When had it changed from needing to rescue someone, to feeling in fact, that he needed to be rescued *himself*, if anything? Her ethereal beauty gave no suggestion of her practical competence. It was there in the way she mastered the horse by her touch and the tone of her voice. It was there in how she walked, unselfconscious, stepping out, looking around as if she was ready for anything, in that bold way of hers.

Tariq had been correct. He'd thought he was rescuing a wounded bird. He just hadn't realized until now that he'd rescued a fierce, tawny hawk, who had a keen physical appetite for everything. He wondered how far it extended. The thought did nothing to quieten his libido.

He pushed himself off the doorway. "Come on. Let's leave the horses until tomorrow. We'll be seeing enough of them then. But now, there are other parts of the castle I'd like to show you."

She kissed the horse on the nose and walked over to him, her head to one side. "Really? And do you think I'll like these other parts?"

"There's food involved."

She grinned. "Lead on."

'Like' was an understatement. They were seated on a patio overlooking the surrounding desert and the trees around the wadi. A warm breeze blew up from the desert, bringing with it the sounds of nocturnal birds. Each side of the patio, tall trees grew, framing the darkened view. Flowers and shrubs tumbled from oversized pots. She adored her estate, but there was no part of it that could compare to the stark glamor and beauty of Qusayr Zarqa.

And Qusayr Zarqa wasn't the only amazing thing. She looked down at her plate and scooped up the last spoonful of the most luscious dessert she'd ever tasted and sat back and sighed. "That was delicious."

"You know, I've never seen anyone as slim as you eat quite so much. You remind me of something."

She tried to contain a smile but somehow she doubted she had, if the sparkle in Sahmir's eye was anything to go by. "Really? What exactly?"

He took a sip of his drink and grinned as he replaced the glass on the table. "A snake. One of those snakes that swallow prey whole."

She laughed. "Charming!"

"A very beautiful snake," he added.

"Too little, too late, I'm afraid, Sahmir. You can't call me a snake and then pretend it's a compliment."

He shrugged. "Worth a try."

He grinned and Rory wondered how many times that charming smile had rescued him from a difficult situation. She doubted anyone could be immune to it—least of all her. She'd been doing her best to ignore the sexual undercurrent all evening. She was beginning to think her best wasn't good enough. She cleared her throat.

"So, do you think I'll be safe from the paparazzi here? Safe from the long arm of the Russian mafia?"

He sipped his champagne before answering and she realized he couldn't vouch completely for her safety. "Safer here than anywhere else. It's remote, no-one knows you're here and you'll have my men with you at all times."

"I'm not safe anywhere, am I?"

"You're about as safe as you can be, here, in a fortress in

the middle of a desert. It would take a Mongol horde to extract you from here."

"Let's hope he doesn't know one." She jumped up, suddenly nervous.

Sahmir rose and went around to her, placing his hands on her shoulders. "It's okay. Don't worry. If Vadim makes a move, I'll know."

"You're having him watched?"

"Of course. Now... sit down and relax."

She sat down but the idea of relaxing was laughable. She shook her head. "I'm so sorry. I brought all this on to you. I'll leave. Just as soon as I can, I'll leave, and your life will return to normal."

He laughed. "Normal? What's that? I don't *do* normal."

"But won't these lies about me hurt your reputation?"

"Of course. But I don't care about my reputation." He sighed. "It's my *country's* reputation, my *country's* future which I care about. And he's aiming to damage that by jeopardizing my marriage to Safiyeh with those paparazzi shots."

"Then, you're right. This is where I'll stay. Out of your way. Out of Safiyeh's way, out of the paparazzi's way."

"That's what Tariq has suggested." He sighed and shrugged. "It's not what I want, Rory, but it's for the best."

"And you think your fiancée will be okay about it?"

"I've spoken with Safiyeh, she understands there's nothing between you and me, that we're just friends."

Nothing. Sahmir was right. Nothing was exactly what was between them, despite the feelings that whirled up from nowhere whenever he looked at her. "Of course. Just friends." She picked up her champagne flute and swirled it around.

He leaned forward as the dark night deepened, his hair ruffled by the warm breeze, his gaze—warm and interested— holding hers.

The flames of the torches that lined the patio flickered,

and the leaves of the tropical plants rose and fell in the shifting currents of air. The terrace looked alive, making *her* feel more alive than she'd ever been before.

He picked up his glass. "A toast. To Aurora, who fell into my life like someone out of a fairy tale."

What was it about him that made her forget everything except the promise he held in his eyes? She held up her glass to his, the bubbles dancing their way to the surface. "To Sahmir, my sheikh in shining armor."

"To 'just friends,'" he added quietly.

Their glasses touched and their eyes met in a moment of quiet that was like a catching of breath in the midst of running a race—a moment when all they'd said felt true. And then they both laughed as if someone had told a joke. Rory didn't know who laughed first. Maybe it was both of them together, but the spell was broken. Whether the laughter was from relief, embarrassment, or from the pleasure of sharing a special moment, she couldn't have said.

But, as they sat back and watched the night settle all around, swapping tales of childhood adventures and misdemeanors, something remained of the moment. It was there in the occasional stolen glance, and it was there in the way Sahmir studiously avoided touching her, as if afraid to scare her away. He was half right and half wrong. She wasn't scared.

No, as they went, much later, to their separate rooms, she thought to herself that there was no way she could be scared of Sahmir. He was the most gentlemanly, most warm man she'd ever met. But she *had* to be apart from him. She had no choice. Whatever he said, her being with him was going to harm his reputation—and his country's—and his future. And she couldn't do that to the man who'd risked everything to save her.

~

When Rory awoke the next morning, it took a moment to realize why she felt excited. Then she remembered and jumped out of bed and threw open the wooden shutters. It was slightly cooler than the day before, and light puff balls of clouds dotted the sky—a perfect day for riding.

It wasn't until after her shower, when she was combing her hair in front of the mirror, that she noticed the bruise on her cheek was beginning to fade. She suddenly realized she'd not thought of the Russian until that moment. Because Sahmir had managed to do the impossible—she actually felt safe here.

~

The blood pounded in her veins, as Rory relaxed into the gallop along the dry plain. She felt as if she were floating, the horse was so good. Hot air rushed by and she was thankful that Sahmir had suggested she wear the red-checkered Bedouin scarf over her hat, wrapped around her nose and mouth to keep out the dust and sand, while the sun glasses protected her eyes.

She was on a level with Sahmir and glanced across to him, at the same time as she reached down and patted her horse's neck. He was totally at ease in the saddle. Despite his lack of interest in horses, he looked in his element. Her competitive streak suddenly emerged and she shouted across to Sahmir, pointing to a tree as she urged her horse on until she was ahead of him.

She eased herself up from the saddle, her slight movement being all that was needed make her horse gallop faster. For several long seconds, she'd thought she'd done it. But then Sahmir moved effortlessly ahead of her, not even bothering to glance at her in victory as they passed the tree. The sleek muscles of his horse gleamed in the light like a well-oiled machine. For all her horsemanship, she was no match for Sahmir.

They continued to gallop, her slightly behind him, across the desert. If there was a path, she couldn't see one. But the horses, and Sahmir, seemed to know where to go. She could just make out a green-grey smudge of an oasis in the mid distance.

They reached it sooner than she'd imagined, the light of the desert making distances deceptive. The horses trotted up to the shade beneath the spreading trees and Rory and Sahmir jumped down. She patted her horse who nuzzled her briefly before following the other horse to the small pool of water at the center of the oasis.

"This is pretty," she said, looking up at the date palm fronds, their leaves shifting only slightly in the light breeze, casting welcome moving shadows on the sandy ground.

"It's called Ein Khadra. It's the nearest oasis to Jabal al Noor."

They followed the horses to the water, where they were drinking contentedly. She leaned back against the rough trunk of a tree and closed her eyes, enjoying the welcome cooling breeze which came to her from across the water. She licked dry lips. "So where's this food and drink you promised me?"

He playfully pulled her hat down over her face. "You're very demanding for a tomboy. Has anyone ever told you that?"

She tipped her hat back up and grinned. "Frequently. With Papa away and Maman not interested in the estate, I organized the workers. They made it quite clear how demanding they thought I was. They did the work, all the same."

"And now you're organizing a Prince. As it happens, I'd anticipated your demands. Follow me." She followed him to a small stone hut that stood on higher ground, a little way from the water, under the shade of a cluster of peach trees.

"Who would live in a place like this?"

"The Bedouin. But it's not inhabited any more. We keep it stocked for ourselves and anyone else in need. I had the supplies replenished this morning."

He opened the door and she stepped inside. It was dark and cool, with few furnishings other than racks upon which were rolled mattresses, and cupboards which no doubt held other things necessary for impromptu overnight stays. But it was a large refrigerator, humming quietly in the corner, powered by solar panels on the roof of the stone hut, that drew Rory's attention. She walked over to it.

"There's no lock." She opened it. "Anyone could access it. Could lift a bottle of"—she peered at the label in the dim light—"Bollinger. I'm surprised you drink alcohol."

"I'm not very devout, I'm afraid. I've lived too long in the west." He walked up behind her and took the bottle. "These are just for us. No-one else would come here." He pointed to other bowls in the refrigerator. "And there's your food."

"Pâté de foie gras, perhaps?"

"Strangely, no. I thought I'd impress you with a little Bedouin style cooking. Some salads and bread. And"—he looked up at her—"wine or water?"

"Water."

"You're so sensible." He passed her the food and bottles of water.

Outside, under the shade of a tree, they sat on stone seats, facing each other as she arranged the food on the weathered table. She sighed as the magic of the place began to penetrate her defenses. She couldn't let it. She'd be gone in a month, if not before. This *wasn't*, and would *never* be, her home, she reminded herself.

She untwisted the lid off the water and drank too energetically, the water overflowing the lip of the bottle and running down her chin. She let it. She was so thirsty and so hot that she ignored the snaking of the water down her top. It was only when she finished that she found Sahmir had yet to begin drinking. His bottle was still poised in mid air, his eyes focused on her and the spreading stain of water on her top. She brushed it away to no effect. The air between them crackled with sexual tension.

He took a quick drink and then placed it onto the table. "Maybe we should wait until it's a little cooler to continue our journey. Maybe have a rest inside the hut."

She shook her head, determined to deny her body's reactions to this man who, no matter what he was doing—playing games with kids, riding a horse, or simply drinking water—appeared to have turned flirtation into an art form. "Maybe we shouldn't."

He shrugged, smiled, and began to eat. "Half-an-hour, then. Something to eat, give the horses a chance to rest."

IN THE END it was more like an hour before they were back on their horses, galloping across the plain toward the site of the gold mine. The tension hadn't lessened despite Rory's best efforts. It was there in every casual glance from Sahmir and every accidental touch as he helped her quiet her horse, spooked by rough ground near the mine as they rode up to the summit of a hill. There they stopped and what she saw put everything else out of her mind.

It was an eerie sight. The massive open-cast mine was silent as a grave. The few pieces of large-scale machinery that hadn't been taken away were motionless, like outsized praying mantises, hovering over the land, about to feed, but frozen in time.

"Wow." It was all Rory could think to say. She'd never seen such devastation. She loved the land, loved farming and to see land laid to waste like this hurt her to the core. She jumped down off her horse and rested on her haunches, gazing out over the destroyed land. "Wow," she repeated.

Sahmir jumped down beside her. "There's not much more to be said. We—Tariq and I—have been working to regain control of this land for a long time. And now we have it."

"And you're going to turn it into a reservoir, you say?" She stood up, pushed back her hat and looked around at the surrounding land. They were standing high above a flat landscape. One way, in the distance she could see the oasis and, beyond that, the desert castle, Qusayr Zarqa, and the other way lay rolling desert fringed by mountains which fell away to a distant sea. Close by she saw groups of cottages, most of which appeared to be derelict, but obviously some people were managing to make a life amongst them. A washing line was stretched, flapping bright colors, between two tumbledown cottages. "It's hard to imagine that this land was once fertile."

"When the wadi is re-diverted back to its original course, it *will* be again." He pointed to one part. "You see the gap in the mountains? That's the original path of the river. It'll flow down here, be contained by the reservoir and from here be pumped out to a system of waterways. It'll bring life back to the desert once more."

She turned from the view to look back at Sahmir. Something had changed. It was in the way he spoke of this land. It really did mean more to him than he let on. "You love it, don't you?"

He nodded but didn't speak immediately. "Yes. But I love many things in life. Unlike Tariq, this isn't all of me."

He turned toward the sun, the light deepening his skin tone, bringing out the depths in his eyes, his white shirt flapping in the breeze that was brisk up there on the ridge. She'd never met anyone like him—not at her home, in the country parties she'd had as a teenager, nor at university in Paris where she'd mixed with men from different countries and different backgrounds to her own. She owed him so much and she'd be leaving Ma'in soon. She suddenly knew what she could do to repay him.

"I can help here, Sahmir. I can *really* help. I know a lot about this sort of thing, believe it or not. I'm sure Tariq is working with the usual international consultants but I have contacts with university academics who are doing advanced research into regenerating the desert. It's cutting-edge stuff. I know it's hard to imagine, but when I look at this I see the potential. I can visualize what it'll be like."

Just at that moment, the sound of a man singing rose from the village below. The hairs on the back of Rory's neck prickled. There was something about the combination of the strange language, the unfamiliar rhythms and cadences that got to her. She lived her life so sure, so practical, and yet here she was in an alien land, listening to music that moved her. It was like the final part of the scene in her mind. People inhabiting and living in a land regained. Sahmir tensed beside her.

"What do you see? Tell me."

She closed her eyes. It was easier to see that way. She waited a few moments as the man's voice rose and fell in a passionate string of words, the meaning of which she hadn't the first clue. All she knew was that it spoke to her and moved her. She swallowed down the emotion. She *wasn't* emotional, never had been. She *wasn't*, she told herself sternly, as the haunting strains of some stringed instrument echoed the rise and fall of the man's voice.

"I see a network of canals, shaded by trees that will

replenish the nutrients to the soil. I see orchards and crops"—the stranger's voice hung on one note before falling away—"and families living there." She opened her eyes. "That's what I see."

"That's what we see, too. When we return to the city you must discuss this with Tariq. You're right. He's working with several agencies to revitalize this place. But he's so distrustful of people. I know he'll listen to you."

"Why do you think he'll listen to me?"

"Because *I* trust you and I'm one of the few people *he* trusts." He took her hand and brushed his thumb over its back. She felt its effect through her whole body. "Thank you."

She smiled at him. "It's the least I can do to try to repay you for what you've done for me."

"You don't have to repay me."

"I do."

He grunted and shook his head. "Okay. You can repay me by sitting here and waiting for a short time. I'd like a few words with the men below. I won't be long."

Before he could turn to go, she pointed to where the mountains petered out into the blue of the sea. "Is that Ma'in over there?"

"No, that's Hadramout. A neighboring country."

She waited for him to continue but he didn't. It was up to her to make the connection. "The country your future wife is from?"

"That's right."

"And those boats out to sea?"

"That's the city and major port. The trade will be useful for the regeneration of this land." He glanced back at the men who were waiting for him. "I won't be long."

Rory glanced once more at the port before walking over to the far side of the ridge. So close to here. It would be within riding distance. She could ride across the desert, across the border and be on a ship, sailing for France, without anyone knowing. An escape route, if she needed it. But if she could easily imagine going one way, what about people coming the other way? Was she really as safe as Sahmir imagined?

She jumped down onto a narrow track, below which a road passed. She looked around but couldn't see Sahmir, or the men. So she continued down the path a little way. Before she reached the road a young Bedouin boy jumped out. She laughed. "You scared me!"

The boy didn't smile. Instead he looked around and seeing no-one around, frowned as if trying to remember something. "The man, he says... he'll see you soon," he said in broken English.

"What?"

The boy frowned harder. "No, he said... soon he'll see... or something."

"What are you talking about?"

The boy shrugged, turned and ran off to a group of giggling boys, jumping like a mountain goat down the mountainside. She tried to follow. But the stones were like scree, shifting underfoot, and she had to move with them, jumping in long leaps down until she reached the bottom of the hill. The boy was nowhere in a sight. He'd somehow melted into the desert. He could be anywhere in the cluster of mine huts, anywhere, camouflaged on the desert, or back in his home.

"Rory!" She heard Sahmir calling her.

"Down here!"

She saw him and he came down to join her. "What are you doing down here?"

She opened her mouth to tell Sahmir, but it was dry with shock. She licked her lips and swallowed. "There was a young boy." She shrugged. "I guess he belongs to the village."

"Rory, what is it? You look as if you've seen a ghost."

She shook her head. She was about to tell him what the boy said but stopped herself. The boy's words were nonsensical as she repeated them in her head. She must have misunderstood. The boy's words could have meant anything. Just a joke amongst boys. That must be it. "Nothing's wrong."

CHAPTER 7

"Rory." Sahmir handed her a drink. "You dressed for dinner. A shameez. It suits you."

Rory felt strangely flattered. She'd wanted to dress up for Sahmir and had chosen the soft pink shameez on a whim. "It's comfortable," she mumbled, looking back at the papers in front of her.

He peered over her shoulder. "What are you looking at?" She tried to fold up the map of the area but he had his hand on it. "The mine?"

She nodded and took a sip of wine. "Just working out what I need to make a start."

"You'll have to talk to Tariq first. He has the engineers to advise him on the reservoir but the advice he's received for the land has been pretty conventional so far, I believe. I'm sure he'll be interested in your views and contacts."

"If my guess is correct, you'll have quite a few options to consider, all of which will help bring life back to the land."

"I can't tell you what that means to both Tariq and myself. Especially Tariq." He rose. "But now, Rory, I suggest you leave your work and come with me." He extended his hand to her and she once more felt her defenses melt a little.

She took his hand. "Where to?"

"Trust me. You're going to enjoy this. I'm beginning to know what you like."

AND SHE DID. The dinner was superb. Course after course of small, tasty plates of Ma'inese cuisine. It was only when the coffee had been served that she rose from her chair and looked around. "This must be the most unusual setting to eat."

"I think the staff would agree. It was a bit of a hike from the kitchens for them. But I always fancied it as a kind of dining room."

"Roman baths as a dining room. Definitely unusual."

"One of a kind. Untouched. Qusayr Zarqa was something my father couldn't get his hands on. It was well and truly owned and run by my grandfather. Tariq has brought it up to date and useable, but, for the rest, he's only let historians stay for a short while. It's never been open to the public, never exploited."

"It's beautiful." She walked over to the edge of the bath which was still and inky in the dark. She gathered her shameez—she was still having trouble getting used to the long skirts—and lifted it to one side and knelt down and put her hand in the water. "It's warm!"

"Thermal. The wadi follows a fault line from north to south through Ma'in." He rose and walked up to the pillars that supported the ribbed, curved roof. "You see here?" He smoothed his hand over centuries-old carvings. "They depict the kind of things the caliphs of old would have done here. Bunches of grapes."

She walked up to him, following the line of his fingers, as

they traced the carvings. "To make wine. For drinking."

"And here, the ibex in full flight."

"Hunting. We hunt on my estate, too…"

He glanced at her with sympathy. She bit her lip. When would she stop calling it *her* estate? Probably never.

"And here"—he turned back to the column—"a feast."

"Such as we've just eaten."

He grinned at her. "*You*, anyway."

She went to punch him playfully but he shot out his hand and gripped hers. He turned it over in his, his thumb smoothing over her hand.

"You're a savage, Aurora. A savage with a fairy tale name and the appearance of an angel."

Her breathing quickened. "Not as savage as you." She looked back at the column he'd been examining and noticed the next sequence of carvings. "Nor your people. Looks like bathing wasn't all they did here."

He followed her gaze at the carving depicting a sexual orgy around the stepped sides of the baths. "Ah, there you have me. My family. My tribe. We had to do something on those long dark nights in the desert."

"You could read a book?"

"Not so much fun." Their hands were still twisted together, his fingers rubbing against hers. "Do you fancy a swim?"

"What here? Now?"

"Why not?"

"Well for one thing, I don't have a bathing suit."

"No-one will come in. I assume you're wearing underwear? That should keep you decent."

She pulled her hand from his and walked over to the water's edge. It looked very tempting. She'd always loved sport, whether it be riding or swimming. She looked back at him. "What about you?"

"I'm prepared to break the habit of centuries and wear clothes." He glanced at the frescoes all around them. "I can feel them frowning at my inhibitions."

"Inhibitions?" She grinned as she slipped off her shameez, revealing a t-shirt and shorts—new and far more decent than any of her old clothes. "I don't believe you have any inhibitions. As far as I can see you possess only one huge flaw."

"Oh, yes? And what's that?"

She stepped onto a ledge, just submerged under the water, creating ripples on the surface of the pool. "You're too damn decent for your own good." Rory's smile died on her lips as she looked up at a face that didn't reflect her own smile. It must have been the shadows in the dimly lit bathhouse that darkened his face temporarily. Only a flicker in the light reflected from the pool as the ripples hit the farther side and rebounded back to her. She looked down, stirring the water with her foot, trying to work out what she'd said that had killed the light-hearted atmosphere. Then she felt a touch on her shoulders.

"You're wrong, you know."

He sat down beside her and she looked back suddenly at her own feet, acutely aware that he was now clad only in boxer shorts and that his naked thigh was nearly touching hers. She suddenly wished the water was cold. She took a deep breath. "I don't think so." She looked determinedly straight ahead at the frescoes on the far wall, and at the light that washed and flickered over them, as the water moved beneath. "Last one in, is a decent human being." She didn't wait for his response but slipped into the water without a splash. It was deeper than she'd imagined and she could only just touch the bottom. She pushed off lightly and turned to see Sahmir still sitting on the side, watching her. She floated on her back on the surface of the water, and watched him watching her. It was the most sensual thing she'd ever done.

They weren't touching, but she could feel his eyes drink her in, every inch of her, covered or exposed. And her body reacted. She briefly caught sight of his body's response before he turned and slipped into the water.

She flicked her feet and swam leisurely away from him to the far wall, upon which the carvings had worn near the water's surface. She loved the feeling of freedom she had in the water.

He didn't make any attempt to swim over to her, but found some kind of seat at the far side and sat, his lower half hidden beneath the surface of the water.

"Ah," she said, moving in the water, enjoying the sensuous slide of it against her body. "Hidden seating."

"You don't think the caliphates and his friends wanted to spend time swimming, did you?" He placed his elbows on the stone wall behind him. "They had important affairs of the state to discuss."

"In here?"

"Of course, in here. And, when they tired of that, there were always the beds, for... *other* affairs."

"Beds?"

He pointed to long shallow, half-submerged shelves, curved to the shape of a body... or two bodies. "They would have been lined with cushions and materials where they could make love in comfort."

She pulled a face as she inspected the area. "But..."

"But?"

"The water, it would have been... would have required... well, changing, not to put too fine a point on it."

He threw back his head and laughed. "You are so wonderfully practical, Rory."

"Hmph." She kicked away again, watching him laugh. She might say practical things, she might *think* practical thoughts, but inside her body was on fire for him. More so, when he laughed like that. There was no suggestion of flirtation, nothing overtly sexual, just him. Being amused. It was more seductive than anything else he could have done. "How deep is it?"

"Deep, at that point."

"I'll find out."

"No! Don't do that!" He'd pushed away from the side and she swam away, laughing, seeing he was about to come after her.

So he wanted to play a game, did he? She'd always been a fast swimmer and she thought she'd easily out-maneuver him, but she'd thought wrong. Within a few strokes, he'd grabbed her foot and pulled her to him. She laughed and tried to dive but he took her by her shoulders firmly and brought her face to his. "No! Rory. I mean it. It's thermal water that's come up from deep in the earth. There's always the danger of bacteria. Don't put your head under."

She'd heard of such things before. It wasn't this news that stilled her. It was his hands on her shoulders, holding her tight. He'd never showed his strength, never exerted his power over her until now... until he needed to protect her. She allowed the pull of the water to drift her body close to his. She bumped against him and then away again. It was brief but long enough for her to realize just how much he desired her. And just how much she desired him.

She exhaled shakily, turned and swam breast stroke back to the side. She pulled herself up and sat on the edge. When she turned he was standing before her. Close.

"Rory, I'm sorry. You're a beautiful woman."

"With very wet clothes on."

"Clothes or not. You're beautiful. I'd have to be made of stone not to react to you. That, I can't help. But I'd never do anything you didn't want me to."

She nodded and smiled. He thought his arousal had

scared her. He was wrong. It was her own arousal that scared her. "Yes, I know." She tilted her head to one side, still nodding, feeling incredible awkward, but also moved. "Because… You are an incredibly decent man." She grinned. "See? I was right all along."

She jumped up and walked over to the pile of towels left on the stone platform and wrapped one around her, aware of the increased transparency of her top. She didn't want to be seduced by him; she didn't need an affair with him. She'd be leaving Ma'in as soon as she could. She'd do the work she said she'd do. But, after that? She'd leave. Because despite what Sahmir claimed, she wasn't safe from the Russian anywhere so she might as well be in the land she loved. No, an affair was out of the question.

She tugged the long white towel tight around her and turned to face Sahmir, who'd slung a towel low around his hips.

"I'm tired, Sahmir."

He nodded too quickly. He knew it was an excuse. "Sure."

"I think I'll go to bed now. But thanks for a lovely evening."

"My pleasure. Is there anything you want?"

She swallowed, unable to take her eyes off the water that gleamed in the dull light as it trickled down his bare chest. There are so many things I want, she thought.

I want you to promise me I'll never see the Russian again. I want to be free to live back on my estate. But most of all, I want you. Now.

She looked up and their gazes tangled for a few heart-stopping moments when she opened her mouth to speak. But no words emerged and she remembered her home, so far from this exotic place. She couldn't complicate things further. She shook her head. "No. No thanks. I'm fine."

"Good. We'll leave for the city early tomorrow. I've

arranged a meeting with Tariq. He's very interested."

"Good."

"And then Tariq and I have a meeting with Safiyeh."

She felt a stab of something like jealousy. "To confirm your engagement."

He paused, his expression unreadable in the dim light. He sighed and looked away. "Yes." He sighed. "Lucky for us, her father and brother are stuck on some airfield in the Far East."

"What are they doing there?"

"Trade negotiations until their plane had engine difficulties. Anyway, after you meet with Tariq, I'll take you to a restaurant I know for our last night together."

She huffed a small laugh. "You make it sound like a romantic tryst."

He was quiet for a moment before reaching out to her and slowly, oh so slowly, running his finger down her wet hair. Then, when she felt she couldn't hold her breath any longer he looked at her with an expression that made her gasp for air. "Isn't it? Just a little?"

She shook her head and stepped away. "No, it can't be. In a few days I return here, alone and I won't see you again. That's the way it has to be."

He sighed. "Yes, of course."

"Right, well, I'm tired. I think I'll go to bed. Goodnight."

She turned and walked out of the bathhouse and padded with damp feet across the ancient hallway.

"Sleep well," he called after her.

She doubted that.

∼

AFTER MEETING WITH TARIQ, Rory had spent the day in Ma'in City immersed in her research. Now it was early evening and Sahmir would be arriving soon to take her to a restaurant he'd told her about. He wanted to show her something of the coast, a contrast to the desert.

She looked up from the computer screen—its scientific facts and figures and graphs beginning to jumble before her eyes—and from the maps that were strewn around the desk, and stood up and stretched. She walked over to the window, pushed it open and stepped out on the small balcony that overlooked the gardens. Despite being a little cramped from working all day, she felt really good. For the first time in a long time, she'd returned to the work she loved, and felt useful. She didn't just *feel* useful, she knew she was being helpful. While Tariq had already hired consultants to begin the transformation from desert to fertile land, he was keen to hear her and her contacts' ideas, and had given her the go-ahead to organize additional research.

Rory had to admit that Tariq hadn't been quite as scary at her second meeting with him. It might have been connected to the fact that she was actually being useful this time, rather than an unpleasant surprise. But she suspected it was more to do with the absence of the woman who'd been a translator at a recent meeting—Cara Devlin—who, it was rumored, had done more than translate. Certainly Tariq's children talked about her as a friend. And even more certainly, Tariq was missing her. She'd catch him gazing out of the window, his mind obviously far away. He wasn't the same man she'd met before Cara's departure.

But, whatever was going on in his personal life, he'd focused on the business to hand and the result was that she was to begin researching on her return to Qusayr Zarqa the following day. She was looking forward to returning there. But she wasn't looking forward to being away from Sahmir. She'd known him such a short time but he was fun to be around.

She inhaled a deep breath of the fragrant air. Who was

she trying to kid? He was *more* than fun. When she was with him all she could think about was *him*. The way he moved, the way he looked, the expression in his eyes when he looked at her—admiring and questioning at the same time. Whatever question he was asking, it was one she couldn't answer.

She sighed and leaned against the balcony, enjoying the view of the garden below which a recently pruned tree now revealed. Suddenly she was aware of whispered voices. Her balcony was at the far end of the building, separate from the rest of the palace. The garden below her would have been the most private part of the garden, especially before the tree had been pruned.

The whispers grew louder. She leaned over the balcony, wondering if it was the children, in which case she'd call out to them. But then she saw them. Hand in hand, the tall man pulling the slight woman, her robes flowing after her as she had to run to keep up with him. Then they turned the corner of a wall and under the privacy of the trees all around them, he pulled her against him hard and kissed her.

For a brief moment, Rory nearly called out, wondering if the woman was there against her will. Her own recent capture created an immediate, visceral response to the scene. But then she saw the movement of the woman, her hands clutching at the man's shirt, her hips pressing in to him, as her lips moved against the man's lips with equal aggression. Rory was frozen to the spot. They were close below her, obviously imagining themselves to be private, unaware that the bedroom above was presently occupied. If she moved, she'd be spotted.

The couple stopped kissing, the man's hands gripped the woman's bottom, dragging up the cloth, while her hands were also busy, out of sight. Rory could see their effect on the man's face, as he closed his eyes and groaned with pleasure. *Mon Dieu*! Were they going to make love down there?

As if answering Rory's thoughts, the man pulled the woman's hands away. "No, not here."

"Then where, when?" The woman's voice was low and urgent.

"When I can claim you for my own."

"You know that can't happen. Not now."

He pulled away, gripping her shoulders, keeping her at arm's length. "You can't keep doing this. You can't do what other people tell you to do."

"I have no choice. You *know* that."

The man turned and Rory gasped. She recognized him. It was Gabriel, Sahmir's cousin—one of the twins who'd been raised in England but had now returned to Ma'in. "How I wish we could turn the clock back."

The beautiful woman softened. Her shoulders drooped and Gabriel brought her to him and held her against his chest, his hands splayed over her back, keeping her close like he never wanted her to leave. "To when, to where?"

"To Cambridge. To the first day we met. To the time I fell in love with you."

It was only when Rory heard the sound of soft sobs that she realized the woman was crying. Her heart went out to her. The woman rolled her head against his chest and then pulled away. "Gabriel, I can't keep doing this. I have to go."

She tried to walk away but Gabriel held her hand. "What if I don't let you?"

"You will," she said softly. "You have to."

"And how can you be so sure?"

"Because you love me, and you'll never hurt me."

His hand relaxed and she withdrew her fingers slowly from his before turning and running from the garden.

Gabriel stood for a few moments thrusting his fingers through his hair before looking up. For one terrible moment, Rory thought he'd seen her. And maybe he would have done, if his vision obviously hadn't been filled with the woman who'd just left. As it was, she was free to observe the suffering on his face and she closed her eyes, feeling the raw pain as if it were her own. When she opened them again, he'd gone.

THE SCENE of the lovers was still preying on her mind when she arrived at the restaurant with Sahmir. Despite the risk of paparazzi, Sahmir seemed intent on taking her out on their last night together.

"You're quiet," commented Sahmir, as he opened the low door of the sports car.

She stepped out into the refreshing sea breeze, the sun low over the horizon. "I was just thinking about your family."

"Why? I'd have thought you'd had enough of them today. Who in particular?"

He offered his arm and she took it as they walked into a long, low building perched on rocks at the end of a promontory.

"Your cousins."

"The twins?"

"Yes. I thought they seemed a little uncomfortable."

"Not surprising after what they've been through."

"Really, what?"

Sahmir shrugged. "Oh, just family stuff. You know."

And she did. Maybe not the particulars, but she had no doubt it would be as complicated as hell, and just as hot. Rory was beginning to understand just how complex the Ma'inese royal family was with its liaisons—illicit and otherwise—and its history of family divisions, greed and overseas takeovers.

She stopped in front of the door. "No doubt they'll settle down. I saw Gabriel with a woman today who he seemed interested in." Interested being a huge understatement. But she reckoned if Gabriel wanted to hide his relationship from the world, that world no doubt included Sahmir. And remembering the pain on his face, she knew she had to respect the couple's desire for privacy.

"A woman? That's unlikely." He considered for a moment. "Who was it?"

Rory shrugged. "I don't know."

"What did she look like?"

"I didn't get a good look at her." But Rory had seen the woman's distinguishing feature—a pure white streak through otherwise black hair. "Why is it unlikely?"

"Because he's only just arrived. He's not been here before and I doubt he knows anyone." Sahmir shrugged. "Anyway, Aurora, may I suggest we concentrate on us tonight?"

"Us?" She tried to suppress a smile but failed. Unconsciously, Rory turned her body from side to side, enjoying the soft swish of the floral silk dress, as soft as chiffon, against her bare legs.

"Yes, us. You look beautiful." Sahmir spoke low, ignoring the fact that the maitre d' was waiting for them patiently by the door that led onto a terrace overlooking the sea.

Rory tried but failed to control a shiver of desire that skittered down her back like a warm breeze. "I *feel* beautiful. I still don't understand how you managed to work out what dress size I was."

A slow smile that could only be described as indecent, spread across Sahmir's face. "I have a good eye."

"A practised eye, no doubt."

"No doubt," he agreed. He let his hand softly trail down her arm and she had to bite her lip to try to prevent a gasp from slipping out, as goose-bumps blossomed under his touch. A flash of desire ignited inside her. Despite her best efforts she must have betrayed her response if the very satisfied look Sahmir had on his face was anything to go by.

It was as if he'd tested her and she'd passed, or he'd passed, and he gripped her hand in his and they walked across the hall, hand-in-hand. As they walked by a wall of mirrors, Rory caught sight of them both and turned away quickly, unable to believe what she was seeing. They looked... simply *right* together. Both tall, he, gorgeously handsome in a perfect bespoke suit and she, well, she'd never seen herself like this before. The dress was a dreamy romantic confection, the high Laboutin heels a revelation for the effect they had on her long legs, and her hair—well, a maid had straightened and twisted her hair into film-star like perfection. She realized that for the first time ever, she'd dressed to please someone. And she could see in his eyes that she'd succeeded.

They stepped out onto the stone-flagged terrace with only the rocks and the sea beyond. She walked up to the edge of the terrace and looked around. The sun was slowly sinking over the horizon and cast a rich light over the bay.

The restaurant was built on a rocky promontory at the farthest point of a horseshoe-shaped bay and the sea was made lively by a warm, brisk off-shore breeze. Small whitetopped waves slapped against the rocky shoreline.

The mangroves that grew on the far side of the bay rose darkly before the setting sun, their lateral roots looking like sea monsters writhing in the shallow water. Beyond them, the city buildings sparkled in the late sun.

She glanced at Sahmir when he came to stand beside her. "What an amazing place. It's so beautiful." She meant to look back at the view but couldn't seem to move her eyes from him.

Sahmir narrowed his gaze as he looked out over the bay and the sculpted planes of his face looked even more handsome in the deepening copper light. He leaned his forearms on the rail that edged the terrace, the quick breeze ruffling his hair and his shirt. If she'd been dressed and primped to look like a film star, it came naturally to him. Then he turned to her and caught her eye, his lips curling into a delicious smile that sent shivers down her spine.

"Nearly as beautiful as you."

That made her turn away. "That, Sahmir, was too glib, too quick off the tongue. Did you say that to the last woman you were here with?"

"I did. And why not? Do you think you've cornered the market on beauty?"

"You're teasing me, Sahmir, and I refuse to rise to the bait. All I'm saying is, don't spin me a line. It won't work."

Sahmir continued to gaze out to the horizon, where the upper rim of the sun was still visible. "Fair enough. It didn't work on my aunt, either."

Rory glared at him but Sahmir met her look with a smile, as he pulled back her chair for her. "Drink?"

"Sure. I think I need one." She looked around the empty restaurant as she sat down. "But where is everyone? Why is somewhere as beautiful as this, so deserted?"

He hesitated, watching the waiter pour the champagne with more interest than he usually showed. After the waiter left he looked back at Rory. "It isn't, usually."

She frowned. "So where is everyone?"

"I booked the place out."

"Just for us?"

He nodded. "Just for us."

"Don't tell me. More photographs of us have appeared?"

"None of you, after all we haven't given them another chance. But they've trawled the old photos of me for the most disreputable ones they could find and added a few of the saintly Safiyeh."

"Your fiancée."

He sipped his wine and shook his head as he replaced the glass on the table. "Not yet." He grinned and she melted a little again. What hope did she stand against him when all he had to do was smile at her?

"So let's see these disreputable photos of you."

"You don't want to see them."

She crossed her arms on the table and leaned forward. "I do." She glanced at his phone and held out her hand. "Show me."

He pushed the phone across the table to her. "I'm putty in the hands of a dominant woman."

She shook her head. "I doubt that." She picked up the phone, pressed the screen a couple of times and was confronted with the image of an inscrutable looking woman who she didn't recognize at first. Her features were stiff, her faint smile formal and her eyes distant and aristocratic. But it was the flash of white hair that gave her away.

Rory turned the phone to Sahmir. "Who's this?"

"That, Rory, is the woman I'm to marry."

Rory couldn't speak for a few moments as the image of Safiyeh and Gabriel in their passionate embrace flashed through her mind. "So this is the…" She frowned. "The—saintly, did you call her—Safiyeh?"

"Yes. She's never put a step wrong, unlike me. A first at Cambridge, no scandal."

Rory fingered the phone, searching the face of the woman, caught by the paparazzi. "Um," she grunted non-committally and handed back the phone. "A hard act to follow."

Sahmir glanced once more at the phone before pocketing it. "Sure is. Anyway, let's not talk of Safiyeh. I have much more interesting things I wish to talk about."

"Is that right?"

"Yes, it is."

"And what do you wish to talk about?"

"Not *what*, but *who*." His attitude of charming playfulness changed in an instant. The smile was gone and his eyes darkened, suddenly becoming intense and probing. "You."

She exhaled shakily. "Surely you know enough about me already?"

His eyes didn't stray from hers. "Nowhere near enough. If I can't have you, Rory, at least tell me all about yourself—your childhood, your family. Your special memories… loves, hates. I want to know everything."

She swallowed as she tried to contain the desire that his words and eyes fanned into startling flames.

"Everything," he repeated. "Fill me up with your words and memories. Anything that will prevent me from turning over the table between us and pushing down those tiny straps which are holding up your dress."

Why was it the breeze seemed to stop, that the air heated up and all she could think about were his hands on her body? "Sahmir, I…"

He shook his head. "Don't try to deny it, Rory. I know desire when I see it. It's there in the flush of your skin, the darkness in your eyes, the rise and fall of your breasts. If circumstances were different, do you know what I'd do?"

She shook her head, unable to utter a syllable, transfixed as he sat forward, leaning his forearms on the table.

"I should take my time of course but truth is I'd be in a hurry to see you without any clothes on. Those breasts"—he shook his head as his eyes dropped to her nipples which she could feel were peaking beneath the flimsy fabric—"I think I've covered every inch of them with my tongue in my imagination." He sighed and she could see the heat had strengthened further in his eyes. "Then I'd—"

She reached forward and placed her hand on his arm. "No! Please don't go on." She sat back quickly, shifting in her seat trying to ease the swollen sensation between her legs. "I'll tell you about my childhood instead." She grinned briefly. "I think it's safer."

He nodded. "Definitely safer. So tell me, did you go skinny dipping in the sea?"

"Sahmir!" she said in a warning tone.

"I'm sorry. It's hard for me to switch gear. But start at the beginning and tell me everything. I need to know you, Mademoiselle Aurora, so I don't ever forget you."

Rory swallowed the lump that had risen at his words and took a deep breath. She'd tell him her life story because she had to admit she didn't want to be forgotten by him.

THE EVENING PASSED QUICKLY and Rory had somehow managed to keep Sahmir at arm's length. Maybe it was the image of Safiyeh—a woman who loved one person but was destined to be with another—that kept Rory's senses about her. That was all it took to remind her that she'd be gone from this place soon, gone from Sahmir. No matter how much she might want to, there was no way she was going to complicate her life further by having an affair with him.

They'd returned in silence from the restaurant and walked up to their rooms, both lost in their own thoughts.

"Goodnight." She began to twist the door handle and looked up at him.

He sighed. "In a different place, a different time, I'd not let you slip through my hands so easily. But here, now, I have no choice but to politely reply 'goodnight' and walk obediently to my room."

"You're about to become engaged."

"Indeed. And my fiancée's family has requested that I do nothing more to stir rumors and gossip about me and you. And there's only one way I can do that."

"Pack me off to Qusayr Zarqa?"

He sighed. "I have no choice. With you here, in the next room, it'll only be a matter of time before, well…"

"Yeah, I know. It's for the best. And you'll stay here?"

"In the city. Working. Being a good Prince."

Despite all she'd said, she felt disappointed. "And you won't be at Qusayr Zarqa at all? Not even to inspect the work at the mine?"

"Don't call it the mine. The Aurus group prosaically called it 'Gold Mine I'. Its real name is Jabal al Noor—Mountain of Light."

"Jabal al Noor," Rory whispered, enjoying the proximity of his face to hers, as much as the feel of the words on her tongue. "Beautiful."

"Yes. You are." Before she could move, he kissed her on the lips. Too soon he pulled away and pushed aside a strand of hair. "Goodnight. And thank you for telling me all about you."

She smiled, trying to lighten the atmosphere. "It was only so you wouldn't forget me."

But his gaze was no less intense than before. "And I won't."

She looked from his lips to his eyes and, mustering all the willpower she could, opened the door behind her and stepped back into the room. He didn't move. Not even when she'd closed the door between them. Not even when she leaned back against the door, listening, aware of his presence on the other side.

It was only when she walked across the marble floor, her stilettos clicking lightly, that she heard his footsteps move down the corridor and the door to his own room open, and then close.

She'd done what she had to do, done what she knew was right. But why didn't it feel right?

CHAPTER 8

There was no sign of Sahmir as she left her room the following morning. She glanced up the corridor but his door was closed and no sound came from his room. He must be in meetings already. Maybe trying to avoid her. For all his attentiveness, it must come as a relief to finally have the woman who'd caused him such headaches out of his life. They'd already said goodbye, but still… she'd hoped she'd see him one last time.

She headed downstairs. The place was unusually empty. She walked up to the door and stood looking out, feeling absurdly disappointed. Sahmir wasn't there. But instead of moving forward to the waiting car, something made her pause and she turned slowly to find Sahmir standing in the shadows, hands thrust into his pockets, leaning back against the pillar—everything about him was casual… except his eyes. She couldn't move under his still gaze.

Then he pushed himself from the pillar and stepped out from its shadow.

"Trying to sneak off without saying goodbye?"

"I thought we'd said goodbye."

"You know? I somehow doubt that." He glanced at the bag she still held. "Here, let me help you with that. All those jeans and t-shirts must weigh a tonne." He gestured forward. "After you."

His eyes burned into her back. His casual stance, the casual words, didn't fool her. She sensed the intensity that lay beneath his conversation, she saw it in the tension in his face and the fierce heat of his eyes.

He handed her bag to the driver and turned to her. His eyes searched her face, just as hers did his. Neither spoke immediately.

"You need anything, just call me."

"I won't need anything."

"Call me anyway."

"No."

"Then I'll call you."

She shook her head but couldn't tell him not to.

"Rory... I—"

"No, you don't have to say anything. I just want to thank you for all you've done. It's far more than you should have done, far more than I deserve."

"I'd do it all again tomorrow. You know that."

She nodded slowly. She *did* know that. Their eyes caught and held—all the words and feelings that neither allowed themselves to express were in that look. It was Rory who closed her eyes first and looked away, shaking her head. "You'd better go."

"I'll see you off first."

"Want to make sure I've gone?" she said trying to lighten the conversation, except he didn't smile.

"You know I don't."

"Your Royal Highness," a voice interrupted.

Rory stepped back but Sahmir didn't shift his gaze from her. "You should go, Sahmir," she said softly. "I'm fine."

Another discreet cough from behind. "His Majesty asked me to remind you about this morning's meeting."

Sahmir sighed but still didn't turn away. "Take care, Rory. I'll call you tonight and, in the meantime, if there's anything you want, phone me."

She nodded, realizing that unless she agreed Sahmir wouldn't leave.

"Promise?"

She nodded again. "I promise."

He nodded. "Right," and turned away with a charming smile to Aarif, Tariq's assistant. "I'm all yours, Aarif."

Rory watched them walk away—Aarif gowned and formal in his manners, Sahmir, hands thrust in his trousers, his eyes roving around the foyer, his hair tousled, casual, as he greeted people. Rory wondered briefly if she'd been forgotten already. Sahmir was the picture of casual insouciance, without a care in the world. And then he turned, no smile, no wave, nothing but a long lingering look that made her stomach flip and tighten with desire. Then he turned a corner with Aarif and was gone.

As Rory turned away she caught a movement in the shadows in the corner of her eye. It was all quiet in the foyer and from out of the shadows a woman emerged. She immediately recognized the streak of white in her hair.

The woman walked over to her with grace and purpose. She was wearing traditional robes, she stood tall and her eyes were wide, serious and intense.

"Mademoiselle Aurora?"

Rory swallowed. "Yes, you must be..." How did she address her? Her Royal Highness? Safiyeh? Sahmir's fiancée?

"I am Safiyeh. Please take a few steps with me in the gardens." Safiyeh's face softened into a hint of a smile, maybe of sympathy, maybe of understanding. Rory nodded, unable to find her voice. Safiyeh indicated the open door.

CLAIMED BY THE SHEIKH

Once in the garden, Safiyeh extended her hand to Rory and Rory took it, looking down at the delicate hand beringed with extravagant diamonds and sapphires. "Please, call me Rory."

"Rory." Safiyeh indicated they should walk and Rory fell into step beside her. "I wanted to meet you before you left."

"Well, I…"

Safiyeh reached out and touched Rory's arm. "It's okay, Sahmir and I understand each other. Ours will be an arranged marriage, purely of convenience for our countries."

"And that's enough for you?" Rory suddenly realized what she'd said. "I'm sorry, it's just that…"

"You don't understand? Of course not, why should you? It's to do with duty and love, love for more than one person. It's not like in the West where one can please oneself."

Safiyeh spoke in a firm, certain tone, and Rory suddenly realized that Safiyeh wasn't the repressed, weak woman she'd imagined. She knew exactly what she was doing and why, and she'd agreed to it. She suddenly understood why Sahmir admired and respected Safiyeh. Like her character, her features were clearly defined—her eyes large and almost fierce looking, her skin, flawless. And, with the streak of white hair, she was stunning. She felt a flicker of jealousy as she looked down at the path they followed.

They walked in silence for a few moments and then Safiyeh stopped and turned to her. "I wanted to thank you for leaving the city, for leaving Sahmir. It'll make it easier for him and for us. But it's not easy for you, I'm sure."

Rory was shocked at Safiyeh's forthrightness and understanding. "I… I mean Sahmir has been very good to me, he helped me, as a friend. He's no more than a friend, you know."

Again, that smile that wasn't a smile lit the eyes, but hardly flickered the lips. Safiyeh touched Rory's arm again gently. "I know you do not sleep together. My staff has informed me of that. And for that, I also thank you. But I also know from how you look at each other that, if it weren't for our impending marriage, your relationship would have become intimate. Your feelings for each other are strong. I could see that in Sahmir's eyes as he said goodbye to you."

"I'm sorry… I don't know what to say."

"You don't have to say anything. I merely wish you to know that I'm indebted to you and if there's ever anything I can do for you, don't hesitate to ask."

"You're not mad at me?"

Safiyeh frowned and her strong brows and intense eyes made her look even fiercer. "Why should I be?"

"Because I've been in Sahmir's company these past few days."

Safiyeh shrugged. "And now you are leaving, so all is well."

"You really don't mind?"

"Not at all, why should I? But for the good of our countries, it needed to stop now. And it has."

The memory of Safiyeh and Gabriel's embrace came into Rory's mind.

"And you're happy with this arrangement? With this marriage?"

"Happiness doesn't come into it. I must obey my father's wishes. I love my father, Rory, very much. My family is close and we work together for the good of the country. My father is not the tyrant he's made out to be in the media. If I really objected to this marriage, then he would not force me into it. Nor would my brother who will be king after my father. My brother is my closest friend. There is just the three of us in our family and we each know our duty and will perform it. I know what I have to do. I know my duty. This isn't about me, not about Sahmir, not about our individual happiness."

Rory was moved by Safiyeh's selflessness.

Suddenly Safiyeh looked up and Rory saw they were standing directly beneath Rory's bedroom, in the same spot Safiyeh and Gabriel had met. Safiyeh looked up at the window and frowned, obviously only just realizing that the spot where she'd met up with Gabriel was overlooked. "I wonder whose window that is?" Safiyeh looked at Rory and Rory could see that Safiyeh was remembering her tryst with Gabriel. Safiyeh shrugged. "What does it matter?" Her beautiful eyes clouded with pain. "What does any of it matter?"

Rory's heart went out to her. A woman who'd willingly deny herself the pleasure of being with the man she loved, for the greater good. "And if there's ever anything *I* can do, please ask," Rory said.

"Thank you. Now I must return, I'm meeting with Tariq and Sahmir this morning. Unfortunately my father and brother are unable to make the meeting because they're still stuck on the tarmac at Thayet airport."

"Thayet?"

"I'm not surprised you've not heard of it. A small country with limited resources. My father has to use his own private plane and unfortunately that has engine problems which will delay him a few days. So it's only me meeting with King Tariq. The formal engagement will have to wait a little longer, until my father returns." Safiyeh paused, looked up at the window once more, looked back to Rory and pressed her lips together in regret. "I have to go. I've enjoyed talking with you. Perhaps in another time and place we could have been friends. I would have enjoyed having you as my friend."

"And I, you. I hope it all goes well for you, Your Royal Highness," Rory said, meaning every word.

"Please, call me Safiyeh." Then she smiled, her first real smile, revealing perfect white teeth, transforming her into an exotic beauty. "After all, that's what friends would do."

Rory waited a few moments and then followed Safiyeh. When she emerged into the foyer there was no sign of Safiyeh, only her driver waiting for her. All Rory's bags had been stowed in the trunk of the car. She walked over and got in, sat back and wondered about the beautiful sad woman with such a fierce sense of purpose and duty.

Suddenly her lot in life didn't look so difficult. A month in the desert awaited her, but it would be a month of interesting work, in a beautiful place with wonderful horses. There were worse things, as she knew... like having the home and country that you cherish more than anything, taken from you. Yes, in a strange way, she understood Safiyeh's choice.

∿

One week later...

SAHMIR CHECKED the plans of the mine against the computer graphics and then looked up at Tariq. "You see, here, there's where Rory's contacts can help us."

The phone rang and Tariq walked over to his desk but turned to Sahmir as he reached for the phone. "Yes, she was spot on in her judgement about the location of the villages." He picked up the phone. "Yes?"

Sahmir continued to look at the preliminary plans Rory and her team had drawn up and had to admit that Tariq was right, the plans would be perfect. "Umm, she knows what—"

"Are you sure?" Tariq's hushed tone made Sahmir stop mid-sentence. He turned abruptly and was shocked at Tariq's expression.

"What?"

Tariq held up his hand to his brother as he listened intently. "Right, of course. And if there's anything we can do… We'll be there as soon as we can. And, Safiyeh, I'm so sorry."

"Tariq? What is it?"

Sahmir was even more worried when Tariq turned to the drinks cabinet and poured them both out hefty whiskies. He gave one to Sahmir.

"Tell me, what is it? Has anything happened to Rory? To Cara?"

They looked at each other for a long moment as they realized what lay behind Sahmir's naming of those women first—the two women who meant most to them, neither of whom were in their lives.

Tariq shook his head. "No. Nothing to do with either of them." He took a swift drink of his whiskey. "It's Safiyeh's father and brother. They're dead. Died in a plane crash."

"What?" Sahmir couldn't believe it.

"They died instantly when the plane didn't make it over the mountains."

"Poor Safiyeh." Sahmir put down his glass and pushed his fingers through his hair as he walked to the window. "Poor girl. She adored them both. But how on earth did it happen?"

"Seems the jet hadn't been fixed properly. Some say sabotage." Tariq shrugged. "Who knows? One thing for sure, it'll unstabilize the situation in Hadramout." He sighed. "Meantime, I've said we'll go to help her as soon as possible."

"Of course."

"The funeral is scheduled for next week."

Sahmir frowned. "But what will this mean?"

Tariq shook his head. "It won't be good for Hadramout, and it could cause instability in the region. We'll be able to better assess it next week when we see Safiyeh."

"And us? Safiyeh and me? I guess it'll be more imperative than ever that we get engaged as soon as possible."

"That's what I think too, but Safiyeh sounded vague,

which is understandable. But she said there were things she needed to discuss."

Sahmir frowned. "Could mean anything."

"And everything. She'll need our help more than ever now."

Sahmir turned away from Tariq, trying to hide his disappointment. For a brief moment he'd thought he might not have to marry Safiyeh. But of course he did. A single woman on the throne would need all the support she could get.

His mind drifted to Rory. He'd be calling her soon. His days seemed to revolve around contacting her. For a brief moment, amidst the shock of the news, he'd allowed himself to imagine a future with Rory. He shook his head. Crazy. Nothing had changed. It had become even more imperative, if anything, that he marry Safiyeh.

He pulled the phone from his pocket and swallowed down the rest of his whiskey. "I've a few things to do and then I'll meet you out the front. I'll tell Aarif what's happening."

As Sahmir walked down the corridor to his suite he suddenly realized that, unless she received violent opposition in her country, Safiyeh would be Queen of Hadramout. And he would be King. There would be no living in Ma'in, no frequent trips to Europe and the States. His heart sank. He felt more tied than ever to a country that wasn't his, and to a woman he didn't love.

∼

One week later...

SOMEONE WAS DRIVING along the desert toward Jabal al Noor. Rory tipped up her hat and narrowed her eyes against the glare. A four-wheel drive from the direction of Qusayr

CLAIMED BY THE SHEIKH

Zarqa. Sahmir? She turned away, not daring to hope, not *wanting* to hope.

She'd not heard from him for a whole week. The first week he hadn't stopped phoning her—morning and evening, and in between. The phone calls had gotten longer, more personal, harder to end, with each passing day. Then, the last phone call, a week ago, to tell her that Safiyeh's father and brother were dead and that he'd be staying in Hadramout for the foreseeable future.

It had been a difficult phone call—stilted and too much left unsaid—and she'd come away feeling numb, as if a little piece of her had died. Sahmir had been trying to tell her that this time, it really was the end of their friendship. And now this?

She turned away from the approaching vehicle and walked along the stony ridge. She'd find out if it was him soon enough. And if it was? He'd probably come to say his final farewells before he returned to Hadramout for good. What other reason could there possibly be?

She turned off the ridge and made her way to the main building where her colleagues and the rest of the large team of engineers and agronomists were based.

She arrived at the offices just as the four-wheel drive pulled up. She jumped down onto the path and ran to greet Sahmir.

Sahmir got out and slammed the door.

"Rory!" He smiled at her with a smile that bridged the weeks.

She smiled hesitantly, unable to let her defenses down quite so easily. After all he'd be gone in a short time—hours, maybe minutes for all she knew. Gone for good, this time. "Sahmir! This is a surprise."

He strode over to her. "It's good to see you."

"And you." The words came out too husky for her liking.

"How have you been?"

She opened her mouth to tell him how she'd been—how *low* she'd been, to be exact—but then she closed it again. She couldn't voice her real thoughts, about how much she'd missed him because it wouldn't be fair. Not to him, nor her. "Fine," she said hastily, desperate to turn the conversation to a less personal subject. "So, you. An unscheduled visit. Any particular reason?"

"Yes," was his only reply.

She sucked in a breath, trying to quieten her beating heart and scuffed the ground with her boots. "Oookaaaay." This obviously wasn't going to be straightforward. He had something to tell her and, unusually for him, he wasn't coming straight out with it. "Would you like to have a look around? It's changed in the weeks you've been away."

"Sure." But he didn't move, only continued to look at her with an intensity that did nothing to quieten the beating of her heart, until finally he sighed and looked around, squinting in the bright light.

"Would you like to meet the others first?"

He frowned as if he had difficulty following what she was saying. "Who?"

"The other scientists. The engineers. They're down there." She pointed to a building under a stand of shady trees, surrounded by swathes of open tents under which people could be seen working.

"No. I mean, later. The sun's getting lower, let's walk."

"Anywhere in particular?"

He looked at her again, his eyes hot. "No. Just away from people."

Her stomach warmed and did a somersault. She drew in a difficult breath. "Okay. Let's walk up to the ridge and I'll show you what progress has been made. And then I'll introduce you to the others. They've got the rough end of the deal, sitting in front of computers, doing all the important stuff."

They fell into step as they walked up the path to the ridge. "While you're outside, no doubt getting your hands dirty with the soil samples, or something or other."

"Good guess. Yes, I'd much rather be outside. Except in the heat of the day and then we're all under cover."

They stepped up on to the ridge, and into a welcome breeze. "The diggers have just about finished, I see," said Sahmir. "It looks a different place to what it was a few months ago."

From their vantage point they could see the whole of Jabal al Noor. All the remaining machinery associated with the gold mine had been removed, replaced with the diggers of the landscapers.

"It won't be long before the river can be diverted back to its original course. The work on the old wadi bed will be complete in a few months."

Sahmir nodded and surveyed the remains of the mine. "And then all of this ugliness will be covered in water."

"And all this"—she turned to look at the desert that spilled out before them like a sea of gold toward the horizon where Hadramout lay, the distant boats just visible in the narrow strip of blue sea—"will return to what it once was."

She looked up at him and he, too, was looking toward Hadramout.

"Have you been here, at Jabal al Noor, all the time?"

"Mainly. I checked out the area as well."

"On horseback no doubt."

"Yeah, any excuse to ride."

He pointed out to the frontier with Hadramout. "I hope you had guards with you and that you didn't go too close to Hadramout? It's safest to keep away from there. I have no doubt that the Russian wouldn't risk crossing to my land, but even so, it's best to stay clear."

She frowned. "The guards come with me everywhere—as you instructed—but I've kept away from Hadramout." She didn't tell him that she'd have done that anyway, even without his warnings. Every time she looked that way she felt spooked, and shivers would track down her spine, as if someone was watching her. She knew it was ridiculous but somehow it always felt better to make sure she wasn't alone.

He looked at her sharply. "And which way, Mademoiselle Aurora, are your thoughts turning to make you look so fearful?"

She shrugged. It was silly to voice a baseless fear. The message from the boy she'd received all those weeks ago could have meant anything, and surely did. There was no point getting Sahmir concerned over something that didn't exist. "I guess it's just that I'll be leaving soon and"—she looked around her—"this place has grown on me."

He reached for her hand and pulled her to him. "Is this the same woman I left at Qusayr Zarqa two weeks ago? Let me see." He tilted her chin and pretended to inspect her face. "Um, a few more freckles, and a deeper tan." He brushed her cheek where there was now no trace of the bruise. "But no bruise. Perhaps all the bruises and hurt have gone now?"

"Just about. Thanks to you."

They were too close now for Rory to hide her thoughts and feelings. And, as the silence deepened, she pulled away, desperate to know. "How's Safiyeh?"

He pressed his lips together regretfully and sighed. "She's devastated but bearing up. She's a very strong woman. She knows what she wants."

Suddenly Rory couldn't bear to hear it. "Yes, I'm sure she does. She can recognize the best when she sees it." She tried to keep the hint of bitterness and jealousy she felt out of her

CLAIMED BY THE SHEIKH

voice, but she thought she'd probably failed if Sahmir's slow smile was anything to go by.

"You did get to know her strangely well in those few moments you spent together." He paused. "Safiyeh told me about your conversation. She's a good woman."

"Yes, well. Anyway, do you want to meet the others now?"

He reached out and placed his hand gently on her arm. "You're right about Safiyeh. She can recognize the best, and she's determined to have it."

Rory bit her lip. Why was he putting her through this? Their brief time together had created an attraction she'd done her best to deny, but the following weeks of phone calls had fanned the flames of her desire, until she was burning for him. Pressure throbbed behind her eyes. God, she couldn't cry. Not here. Not with Sahmir. "I know, Sahmir. You've told me all about it. And—" She blinked her eyes, the tears apparently determined to appear, even in the dry heat of the desert. "*And*," she repeated, firmer this time, "I don't want to hear any more. You're about to marry her—"

"I'm not," Sahmir said quietly.

"And I wish you both well. I really do. Safiyeh is—"

Sahmir gripped her arms. "Rory, listen to me. Safiyeh and I *aren't* getting engaged, married, or in any way connected."

She whirled around to face him. "What? But you said…"

"I said a lot of things. Things based on Tariq and my assumption of what Safiyeh would want, what she'd need."

"And she doesn't need you?"

"No. She's going it alone. She has the support of the government and good advisers and she wants to try it alone."

"Ah." Rory remembered the expression on Safiyeh's face as she looked up at Gabriel. While she was sure Safiyeh would want her father and brother brought back to life in a heartbeat, she was also sure that Safiyeh had decided that she'd make her own decisions from now on, including who she'd marry. She looked up at Sahmir and smiled, raising her eyebrows. "So, where does that leave us, Prince Sahmir?"

Sahmir released his grip on her arm and took her hand instead. "Wherever you wish, Mademoiselle Aurora." He swept his finger across her cheek. "A speck of dust."

She narrowed her eyes. "A speck of dust? Really?"

"Of course! Do you think I'd use that old line to touch your face"—he raised his finger again to her face—"to trace the line around your eyes—which, by the way, are a quite disturbing shade of blue—and then over your cheek bone, down into the hollow of your cheek—um, like silk—coming to a stop at the corner of your lips?"

"I think you might."

He narrowed his eyes and their sexy intensity registered in her belly, and lower. "And why is that?"

She moved her face so that his finger was no longer at the corner of her lips, but on them. She opened her mouth and licked her lips, at the same time licking his finger. "Um, I think you might, because my mind was going along a similar path."

"Really?" He inhaled a long breath. "And where does this path end?"

"That, Prince Sahmir, is an impossible thing to answer."

"Then maybe we should begin along that path and see where it leads?"

What the hell was she thinking of? 'Nowhere' was obviously the answer. Then she found herself nodding in agreement.

"Mademoiselle Aurora, would you care for a lift back to Qusayr Zarqa?"

She shouldn't. "I would."

CHAPTER 9

It was late by the time they'd finished talking with the scientists and were back on the road to Qusayr Zarqa. The sun had set and the short dusk was drawing to a close. They were passing the oasis when Rory asked him to stop. They parked up in a cloud of sand and dust.

"Why did you want to stop here?"

She couldn't really have said. "I haven't been here since that day with you when we stopped off to let the horses drink."

"Would you care for a drink yourself? I have more than just water on offer. I persuaded one of the engineers to hand over a bottle of Moet. Besides, the oasis in the moonlight is a magical place."

"Sure. Why not? But there isn't any moon."

"Not yet."

With the moon yet to rise, it was darker under the spreading canopy of trees. Rory shivered, partly wondering what on earth she was doing, and partly because she knew exactly what she was doing.

When they came to the water, the darkness gave way to light as the water reflected back the sky that still held a memory of the setting sun, and the stars which were beginning to prick through the darkening blue. It was cool after a hot day and Rory felt an urge to dive in. "Can we swim in it?"

"Not in the oasis itself but there's a small pool where the water has been diverted for just such occasions. Come on, I'll show you."

As they walked carefully around the oasis to behind the stone hut, she saw what she'd failed to see on her previous visit—a newly built spa pool off to one side of the pool itself. She peered inside. "It's empty."

"That's what pumps are for."

She sat on the side looking around her, thinking how strangely at peace and happy she felt, while Sahmir disappeared into the hut and the hum of a motor started. Sahmir was still inside the hut as water began to fill up the pool. Quickly she stripped off her clothes, leaving on only her bra and panties, and jumped into the pool. She gasped at the slight chill against her hot body. She found a seat and then sat down, allowing the water to rise gently over her body.

Sahmir emerged with a bottle of champagne and two glasses. He still wore trousers—she immediately noticed—but no shoes or socks. He looked even more gorgeous half-dressed. The thought flitted through her mind how much more gorgeous he'd look naked.

He glanced down at her pile of clothes and looked at her. "Are you naked in there, Mademoiselle?"

She looked up with a grin. "I considered it, but no."

"Please, don't keep on your underwear on my account. Besides, it's quite dark, I'm sure I'll hardly notice."

She laughed. "No way."

"Here." He held out the bottle and glasses to her. "Hold these while I join you."

She was about to answer when he began to undress. She looked straight ahead. Thank God for darkness.

She watched as his outline joined her at the far side of the pool. The water had stopped pumping and now washed around their chests. Rory sunk down a little to cover her breasts.

"*Shucram!* Rory. Thanks for all you've done. I never thought I'd say this, but I'm glad that you ran down that snowy street and into my arms."

She laughed. "Not *exactly* into your arms."

He sipped his champagne. "This is no time to be a stickler for the truth. Look at those stars. It's far too romantic."

She took a sip of the wine, enjoying the sensation of the bubbles tickling her throat and the headiness of alcohol after nothing but soft drinks and water for weeks. "*You* are far too romantic. I can't forget the events that led up to that moment. That, that… *man.*" She shuddered, unable to elaborate. With just those words the atmosphere changed.

"Did he force himself on you, Rory?"

"What?" For a minute she couldn't think what he meant. Sahmir was usually so cool and unconcerned about things that the seriousness in his tone made her suddenly realize what he wanted to know. He really wanted to know whether she'd slept with the Russian. "You mean, me, the Russian. Did we…"

"Well, yes. The more I know you, the more I can't bear to think of you with him, having to submit to him."

She shook her head. "No. I told you before."

"I wasn't sure. You may have been saying it for some other reason."

"No. I was saying it because it was true. He tried to have sex with me. He tied me up." Her hand automatically went to her wrist where the marks had been. "You know that. You saw the ropes; you've seen the marks on my wrists."

"Yes." The clipped answer revealed the anger that lay behind the one-word reply.

"But he couldn't... he couldn't do anything. That's why he lashed out and hit me."

"But the other men. They seemed to think..."

"Because he told them that he'd... you know." She suddenly felt shy about stating exactly what the Russian had told his men. "He wasn't about to tell them that he wasn't able to have sex."

Sahmir sighed and he shifted in the pool, the water lapping around her. "I can't bear the thought of you with him."

She continued to look at the stars. She couldn't look at him. If she did, she wouldn't be responsible for her actions. She took another quick sip of wine. Followed by another. The glass was suddenly empty.

At that moment the moon rose behind the mountains, filtering its light through the trees.

They turned to each other and she could see him completely for the first time since they'd entered the oasis. Gone was the flirtatious looks, the smile. He was looking at her with a longing she reciprocated and which she knew would be plain to see.

"Rory."

"Sahmir, I..."

His eyes slipped down to her breasts, clearly visible through the wet bra, and she sank down into the water. He looked back up again, amusement now in his eyes. "Looks like you're out of champagne. Would you like some more?"

She bit her lip and nodded. He stretched out in the water and topped up her glass before sitting down beside her. He slid down and rested his head back against the smooth rock.

She took another sip of champagne and placed the glass down, realizing too late as a sensuous lethargy overtook her, that she was drinking too fast on an empty stomach. She sank under the water and stretched out, relishing the feel of the warm water against her skin. She sighed and laid her head back so she was looking up at the night sky. "What are you looking at?" she asked.

"The stars."

She pointed up to a particularly bright star. "You have pretty stars in Ma'in." She fluttered her fingers. "Twinkly."

He looked at her sharply. "Are you tipsy, Mademoiselle Aurora?" he said in a mock-stern voice.

"Not at all," she replied indignantly. "Well," she said as she reconsidered. "Maybe a bit. But that doesn't make that star up there any less twinkly."

"I believe stars twinkle the world over."

She ignored him. "What's that one called?"

"Ibet al-Jauza."

She glanced at him, impressed. "What a lovely name."

He laughed.

"What are you laughing at?"

"It translates as 'Armpit of the Central One'."

She laughed and pointed to another one. "And that?"

He narrowed his eyes, as if her question was stretching the limits of his knowledge. "That's a planet, I think you'll find. Al-zahra, or Venus as you'd call it."

"Wow, I prefer your name, it's beautiful!" She waved her hand to another. "And that?"

He didn't even bother to look at the stars now. He was gazing intently at her arm instead. "Al-zahra the Second."

"You didn't even look to where I was pointing!"

He shrugged. "One star, one planet, is much like another."

"You've been making up the names!"

"Maybe. They sound vaguely familiar. I'm sure they're the names of something or other."

She grunted and sat up, bringing her face close to his. He

leaned forward, accepting the implicit challenge. "Something or other? What kind of Prince are you not to know the names of the stars over your country?"

"They're your stars too!"

"Yes, but we call them different names."

"Not so very different. Most of them are derived from the Arabic names."

"Really?"

"Yes, really."

She sighed and sank back under the water, then jutted out her lower lip and blew upward to remove the hair that was falling on her face.

He leaned across and lifted the offending lock of hair, laughing as he did so.

"You, Prince Sahmir, are laughing at me."

"Only a little."

"Well." She leaned over, about to poke him in the chest. "I won't have it." But somehow she slipped and he grabbed her shoulder. And when she lifted her head it was close to his. His lips. So close... Somehow it required no further movement of hers before their lips met.

She didn't know who was more surprised—him or her. What had begun as a playful gesture turned into something completely different in an instant.

As soon as her mouth touched Sahmir's, it was like striking a touch paper. Passion flared between them and he opened his mouth under hers as she found his tongue with her own. Her body melted against his and his hands slipped around her bare back before resting on her waist, no further, as the kiss deepened.

When at last their mouths parted, she pulled away. "I'm sorry. I don't know how that happened."

He laughed and reached for her hand and kissed it. "Rory!

I do. I've been wanting to kiss those lips of yours since the moment I first met you."

"Really? Is that why you rescued me and brought me to Ma'in?"

"No, of course not. I'd have helped anyone in your predicament—whether or not they had lovely lips." He paused. "But I'd have drawn the line at kissing them." He shrugged. "Actually, I might not have brought them to Ma'in." There was a long silence. "And I wouldn't be sitting in this pool with very few clothes on with anyone who had unlovely lips."

She sank back under the water. "So my lips saved me. Who'd have thought they could be so powerful?"

"I've never had any doubt that yours would be. And I was right. Just then, the way they moved against mine."

The low spreading warmth probed further in Rory's belly and elsewhere. She shifted on the stone seat, suddenly very aware of a needy ache between her legs. "I'm not sure what you mean."

"Really?" With a whoosh of water he was seated beside her. "Perhaps I should show you."

She opened her mouth to answer but before she could speak his mouth was on hers and all thoughts, all words, fled from her mind. Everything was centered in the movement of his lips against hers, his breath in her mouth, his tongue touching hers, turning her insides liquid. He pulled away too soon.

"You were wrong," she said with difficulty, as she tried to keep her breathing even. "It's not my lips. It's yours that have the power. The power to make me forget everything."

"Including that you're practically naked?" He brushed his lips against hers. "And that your hands are around my neck, and your breasts are pressed against my chest?"

She looked up startled and pulled away, sinking under the water once more. "Yes. I rest my case."

She closed her eyes against the stars as his fingers trailed up the side of her leg, her hip and up to her stomach. "Would you like another drink?"

She shook her head. She daren't speak, fearing it would come out as a moan of ecstasy.

"Do you want to go back to Qusayr Zarqa?"

Again she shook her head.

"What then?"

She gripped his hand as it drew a light line around the top of her bra, over her rapidly falling and rising breasts. Briefly, she held it in place and then, her hand holding his, she moved it until the flat of his hand extended over her breast, with only the soaked, flimsy material of her bra between her flesh and his. It was his turn to close his eyes.

"Oh, Rory." He moved closer, his lips finding hers once more, as his hands slipped under her bra and caressed her breast.

She gasped under his mouth and turned under his body as he pressed against her. Her legs opened naturally against the press of his thighs and she slipped from the seat and they both sank suddenly under the water, coming up spluttering and laughing. He kissed her once more.

"Let's get out of here." He brushed his warm lips against hers. She opened hers in readiness. He touched her lips with his finger instead. "Come." He rose and water fell from him, over his shoulders, chest, stomach and lower, to where his shorts did nothing to cover his arousal. She stood up and he took her hand and helped her out. She stumbled over the stony ground and was immediately swept up into his arms.

She snuggled against his chest. "Um, you smell nice," she said as she sniffed his skin.

He laughed. "You're like an animal, Rory, an animal

sniffing me out to see if I'm attractive to mate with." He laughed again as he kissed her neck and his tickling breath sent shivers down her spine. She wriggled in his arms, his hand tightening under her bottom. She wriggled again and turned her head up to his, bright now in the moonlight.

"How come you always seem to end up carrying me around?"

"I'm just that kind of man, I guess. Passing over your everyday kind of girl who can walk, and instead finding myself irresistibly drawn to a woman who can't, or won't."

"Um." Burying her lips and nose against his chest once more. "Irresistible, am I?" she murmured as she feathered kisses across his skin.

He looked down at her, his eyes intensely sexual, so close to hers. "You know you are."

"I know nothing of the sort. But… I'm not about to argue with you because I'd like to be irresistible to you."

He stopped at the entrance to the stone hut. "Really? And why's that?" He relaxed his hands and she stood, leaning against him, feeling every inch of his hard body pressed against hers.

"Because I want you to make love to me." She felt his response as a groan that traveled through his body and into hers—one of desire and frustration. She wriggled lightly against him, and his hands smoothed over her wet knickers and cupped her bottom, drawing her yet closer to him. "Here, now."

"I'd love to oblige but we have no condoms. I borrowed the champagne from one of the engineers and didn't like to enquire about condoms. I was thinking of your reputation."

She smiled as she kissed his chest. "No, that wouldn't have been a good look. But… we could sleep here anyway. It's so romantic, the oasis… the stars… the empty desert…" She swallowed as she tried to rein in her desire. "Besides, we're both sensible people with self-control. We can make sure we don't go too far."

"I believe, Rory, that you could persuade me to do just about anything." He exhaled softly and wrapped his arms around her, bringing her close to him, brushing his lips against hers. "Let's celebrate self-control. And we can begin by making up a bed for us, under the stars. We've everything we need in the car." He kissed her again. "When I say everything, I have a couple of blankets."

"Just blankets?"

"Yes. That's all we'll need. One to lie on and one to cover us... after..."

"After?"

"After I've kissed every inch of your body. After I've made love to you without making love."

WHILE SAHMIR WENT to get the blankets, Rory walked to a place where three trees stood in a protective semi-circle around a small clearing. The only sound other than Sahmir closing the car door was the rustle of the palm fronds overhead and a hoot of an owl. She looked up into the night sky where the moon had risen, its light dimming the stars, reached behind her and unhooked her bra, and tossed it to one side.

She wanted to be naked when he came to her. She wriggled out of her panties and threw them on top of her bra. If Sahmir was holding back because of a lack of condoms, she wasn't. Unless she was traveling or under stress, her periods had always been as regular as clockwork. She was as safe as houses. She wanted him and she was going to have him.

She closed her eyes and felt her flesh goosebump, and her nipples peak, not because of any chill in the air, but because of the awareness that Sahmir had just entered the glade.

She heard the soft thud of the blankets as they hit the ground and then he was before her. His hands moved up the sides of her body and around her breasts, caressing them, as his lips found hers. She wrapped her arms around him, bringing his body hard against hers. Their breathing was coming hard and they parted.

"Oh, Rory," he muttered as his lips found her neck and lower, down to her breasts. He lifted them both until their fullness was accentuated and he took first one into his mouth and suckled, and then the other.

Ripples of pure pleasure flowed through her body, increasing her need further. She tried to push down his boxer shorts but he placed a firm hand on hers as he kissed her on the lips once more. "Take those off and all bets are off. Now, lie down." His voice was gruff and commanding and she had no other thought but to obey.

She sat on the blanket and her eyes drifted along his long, leanly muscled body, to his shorts that covered too much of what she wanted to see. "Now what? Would you like me to help you with your shorts?"

"No! I want you to behave. Lie down and let me look at you."

She settled back, casually shifted her arms under her head and looked up at him. If he thought he was going to be the boss around here, he had another thought coming. She neatly crossed her ankles. She knew he liked what he saw when the silk of his boxers moved. He wanted her as much as she wanted him, deep inside her.

So instead of being obedient, she sat up and knelt before him and dragged her nails up the back of his legs, circling behind his knees before slipping swiftly up under his boxers and pulling them down. Before he could stop her she brought her hands around his erection, smoothing over his skin, with her fingers searching out the shape and texture, with her fingertips teasing the tight, heavy sac at the base.

He muttered words she didn't understand as she slipped him into her mouth, tasting him, sucking him into her mouth as far as she could, before withdrawing and licking the end which glistened in the moonlight. It was her turn to groan. As much as she enjoyed exploring his body with her tongue, she wanted what she was holding in her hands somewhere quite different.

She slipped her hand between her legs, feeling herself so wet for him and raised her damp finger and smoothed it over him. Then she looked up at him. He'd been watching her every movement. He shook his head. "What are you doing to me, Rory?" His voice was hoarse with need.

"I'm seducing you." She rose to standing, held his erection in her hands and rubbed it against her. She gasped and closed her eyes at the intensity of pleasure it brought. She raised one leg which he caught with his hand, as she moved him closer to where she wanted it, slipping it up and down her slick folds, as she kissed him, her tongue circling first his lips, and then inside his mouth.

He pulled away first, his eyes fierce with need, as he lifted her up into his arms and slid deep inside her, his eyes never moving from hers. She closed her eyes and gasped as his heft and length filled her completely.

Still connected, he carried her over to the blanket, their mouths finding whatever skin there was, kissing, tasting, as she clung on tight.

They moved to the ground as one. He drew her hands out and gripped them above her head and eased out of her body. She wrapped her legs around him, lifting her hips up and he pushed deep inside her once more.

With each thrust into her, the tension spiraled until she could hold on no longer and her loud cries filled the night sky. He stifled her cries with his mouth and then pulled out and rolled onto his back.

She didn't miss a beat and immediately rolled on top of him and sat astride him.

"Rory," he warned.

She smiled and leaned forward so her breasts hung in front of his lips. He groaned and tasted first one breast and then the other, drawing her nipples out hard. He withdrew his mouth and lay watching her as her hands busied themselves with him. She shifted and was about to push on top of him, when he gripped her hips tight so she couldn't push herself back onto him.

"No!" she cried, desperate to have him inside her.

"We can't, Rory. We have no condoms with us."

She didn't want to hear anything about what they should or shouldn't use. All she knew was that she wanted nothing to come between them. In that moment she just wanted to be his woman, fully and completely. To give herself to him for all that he'd given her and for all that he could give her.

"No!" she said more firmly still, taking him in her hand and rubbing him against her wet folds.

Again those muttered words which, although she didn't understand, knew their meaning. She sat up and slowly slipped over his length until he was fully inside her. She sat, her eyes closed, allowing the delicious sensations to wash through her body. Then he shifted slightly and exquisite sensations shot through her. She moaned and gripped his shoulders, opening her eyes to see his eyes full upon her, drinking her in.

His skin was dark, shaded from the moonlight by her body, as she rose and fell against him. The only things that were bright were his eyes—the most indecent part about him. It was the most erotic thing she'd ever seen. She gripped his shoulders harder as she lifted herself up and then down, repeatedly, her hair moving over his shoulders and chest, her lips and breasts hovering just above him, dipping and nearly touching and then away from him again. His hands were around her hips, but not restraining her any more, guiding her, holding her still and then releasing her in time to her own rhythm... and his.

Sensation held complete mastery over her body and mind. She was like a slave to the feelings his body created in hers. Her whole world was focused on this one moment, this one sensation that held her body in complete thrall. On she went, shifting up to the end of his length, moving lightly before plunging down on top of him, taking him all inside her, rewarded by a look of pained bliss as he closed his eyes briefly.

His hands left her hips, allowing her to do whatever she liked and he caressed her breasts as she continued to move, the coiling sensations increasing inside her. Her movement grew faster until she was pumping on top of him and she cried out loud as she was overcome with a mind-blowing orgasm. She collapsed on top of him and he wrapped his arms around her and kissed her.

Slowly her breathing returned to normal and they rolled side by side. He pushed her hair from off her face and kissed her and then he began to withdraw.

"No!" she wriggled further onto his hard shape. "Don't go."

"This isn't right."

"But I love the feel of you." She reached down and stroked around and under him, pulling herself off and then back onto him again.

He groaned. "Much more of that and there'll be no going back." He pulled out of her. "No, Rory." But she was insistent, touching, kissing, moving against him, making him want her as much as she wanted him. And it worked.

He groaned, rolled her onto her back and thrust into her. She lifted her hips and wrapped her legs around him and hung onto his shoulders as he slammed into her relentlessly and repeatedly until he came. She moved her hands to his bottom, feeling the small thrusts as he shot his seed deep inside her.

He muttered something incomprehensible and rolled off her, kissed her completely and masterfully and then withdrew. "Rory..."

She snuggled closer to him. "Yes?" She smiled against his chest, kissing him. It felt so right being in his arms, her body nicely tired, her mind for once quiet.

He sighed and her name was exhaled on that sigh "Rory..."

She'd drifted away and opened her eyes suddenly. "Um?" Her mind drifted away again and she opened her eyes, before letting them flutter and sink closed, and her breathing fall into his rhythm—the pattern of sleep.

The night passed in a haze of love-making and sleeping until she awoke in the early morning light to find Sahmir sitting, half-dressed, watching her.

"So much for self-control," he said. "I'm sorry, Rory. I shouldn't have—"

She rolled over and stopped him talking with her lips. "Don't apologize. It was my fault. You were being all gallant, and would have had self-control if I hadn't forced myself on you. I apologize. For all my big words, I've never been big on self-control. My mother has always said I'm far too headstrong for my own good."

"So I shouldn't have believed you when you said you were a sensible adult."

"Not at all, I'm afraid." She reached for his hand. "I guess it was wishful thinking on my part." She sat up.

"If you want to bathe, there's a portable shower fixed up outside the hut."

"Perfect."

She walked over to the hut, tugged the shower on and stood under it, turning under the warm water, vaguely feeling she should feel guilty, ashamed, or something. But she didn't. All she felt was hungry for more.

~

THEY ARRIVED at Qusayr Zarqa before dawn, drawn by the lure of condoms. Sahmir drove straight into the garage.

"Now, Rory." He began covering her up. She moaned and ran her hand up his leg. He swore and dragged her hand away. "Rory, focus." He pulled her scarf around her. "There will be staff everywhere."

"But I want you."

He kissed her much longer than he'd meant to. And when he pulled away he was back to square one again, with the zip of Rory's shorts open and her top undone. He vaguely remembered opening her buttons. He kissed her again, more chastely this time. "Once we're past the servants we can do as we like."

She sighed. "You mean you don't want me walking through the hall, half dressed, looking as if I've just made mad passionate love in the desert."

"Exactly. You've got it." He adjusted her top, patted down her hair ineffectually and laughed. "Somehow I think they're going to guess anyway. I can't do anything to hide the expression on your face, nor those lips." He pressed his finger against them as he frowned. "Swollen lips." He swore again.

She grabbed hold of his shirt and held him close to her. "I know I shouldn't have insisted, but making love to you like that was... well, perfect."

His face softened. "It was. But it shouldn't have happened. Not without a condom."

"No. But I can't regret it."

He kissed her. "Nor me. Now, let's get up to the bedroom. There are plenty of condoms there."

In one swift move she adjusted her clothing, grabbed her things and stepped out the car door.

MUCH LATER THEY LAY, side by side, listening to the morning sounds of the castle going about its daily routine, and Rory shifted her arm that lay across Sahmir's chest. She'd thought he was asleep until he grabbed her arm again and replaced it on his chest, patting it once and leaving his hand there so she couldn't move it again. And she didn't.

As Sahmir's breathing slowed into sleep once more, Rory shifted her other hand behind her head and looked out, across the room, through the arched window that followed the treed wadi, its blue-green a more vivid color early in the morning. It really was a beautiful place. But it wasn't home. Not her home. And it never would be.

When she'd first arrived in Ma'in, she'd been relieved. She'd escaped the Russian. All he'd been able to do was have a few photographs of them taken and published. Nothing more. She was beyond his reach here. Even now, with the confidence of hindsight, she knew that she'd never have managed it on her own, never have got out if it hadn't been for Sahmir. She turned her head to look at him.

He was such a kind man, so fun, so loving and so damned sexy. She still didn't really understand how he'd been able to arrange a late night gambling session with the Russian at the last minute. Sahmir had told her that when he'd discovered she'd been taken from the hotel, he'd arranged a game with the Russian. She'd taken his words at face value, but now she began to wonder how on earth he'd been able to do that at such short notice.

She sighed. No doubt someone with Sahmir's royal connections could do anything. Even without the connections, she thought tenderly as she admired his handsome features, he'd be able to sweet talk anybody into just about anything.

"Stop looking at me like that." He opened one eye.

She propped herself on one elbow, continuing to look at him. "How did you do that?"

"I'm extremely clever." He sat up in bed, and gave her bottom a brief squeeze before standing up and stretching. "Best you should know that about me, before you consider fooling me. Now, Mademoiselle Aurora. Time to rise. We've a long day ahead."

"So long as we're outside on horseback and there's lots of food, I'll be fine."

She got up and gave him a hug, pressing her naked body lightly against his. His reaction was immediate. She raised an eyebrow as she looked down, then back up at him, as she backed away. He made a grab for her but missed. "Okay, my extremely clever Prince. Sort that out. I'm off for a shower." She only just closed and locked the door before he got to her.

"You wait. I'll get you back."

She laughed as she flicked on the shower. She was sure he would. And she was equally sure she'd like it.

RORY HAD NEVER FELT QUITE SO tired, or quite so relaxed, so... sated.

The bathroom door was pushed open and Sahmir emerged, a towel slackly tied around his waist. "Look at you, Rory! You look like a love goddess."

She glanced down at her body, naked except for a white

sheet twisted around one leg. She wriggled her bottom. "In that case, I think you should come over here and worship me before I go and have another shower."

He shook his head, laughing, as he reached for his shirt. But she could see from the movement under his towel that her words had had the effect she wanted. "You, Mademoiselle, are insatiable."

"I disagree. I think one more time should do the job."

"No. I have meetings this morning in the city. I've no time."

She pouted, the challenge of his words giving her the energy she needed. She rolled onto her stomach and, as he passed by the bed, she reached out and grabbed his towel and threw it across the room, leaving him with only an open shirt and a very hard erection. "Come here, I can help you with that."

She reached out but before she could touch him, he grabbed her, rubbed his hands over her bottom, slipping under her hips and pulled her to him.

She cried out in surprise and then yelped as he maneuvered her bottom against his body and she felt him pressing at the place where she wanted him, between her legs.

"You, Aurora"—as he thrust inside her with one swift movement, turning her laughter into moans—"are *one*"—he thrust again, emphasizing his words—"very"—another thrust—"naughty"—another thrust—"woman"—another thrust.

Each thrust brought her nearer to the edge and then he stopped, deep inside her, as he played with her from the front with his fingers. She gasped and squirmed against him. And then he withdrew his fingers.

"I'm sorry," she gasped out, "what did you say?"

He repeated his actions not once, but twice. She felt he could have continued all day. But she didn't need him to. With the final thrust inside her they both came and they rolled onto the bed together. She, wrapped in his arms, still with her back to him.

He caressed her stomach and breasts as he kissed her neck and back. "I have to go. But I'll be back tonight."

He rolled off the bed and went to the bathroom.

The word 'tonight' warmed her and she rolled to her side and looked out the window at the bright sky. There'd be a tonight and a tomorrow with Sahmir. And who knew what possibilities after that. She sighed, closed her eyes and drifted off to sleep.

∽

Two days later...

RORY LOOKED down at Sahmir sleeping and thought she'd never been so happy. He was as physical as she was… as insatiable as she was. As each day passed, her feelings for him grew, despite her trying to hold them in check. After all, she wasn't going to be here forever.

She missed her family. She spoke to them often and knew they were safe and as happy as possible. But, as each week passed, and there was no progress on regaining her estate from the Russian, her determination to return to Europe—whatever the risks—increased. She looked at Sahmir again. And as each day passed with Sahmir, her feelings for him deepened, adding to her confusion.

She kissed him and, for a moment, wondered whether she had time to wake him up. But one look at the clock put pay to that idea. She had work to do.

She swung her legs off the bed.

"Where you are going so early?" Sahmir stretched out a sleepy hand and caught hold of Rory and pulled her up short.

"It's all right if you're a Prince, but *some* people have to work around here, you know." She bent down and kissed him.

"Well," he said when she'd summoned up all her self-discipline and managed to pull away. "At least let me watch you dress."

She shot him a look and walked to the bathroom. "No way. I know where that would lead."

"Back to bed?" he offered hopefully.

She nodded. "And I don't have time. I said I'd take some soil samples out by the bend in the old wadi."

Sahmir sat up in bed and frowned. "I hope you're not going alone."

She shook her head. "I remember what you said. 'Always take armed guards.' And I do."

Sahmir grunted but didn't look any better pleased. "It's more important than ever now. The old wadi runs close by Hadramout. Safiyeh is doing her best but the country is on the verge of chaos." He swung his legs off the bed. "I'll come with you."

She turned to him and looked him up and down in a leisurely fashion. It had its effect. He went to grab her but she stepped away. "If you come with me, neither of us will get any work done. It's fine. I've arranged for three of the guards to come with me. Don't fuss. I'll be fine. You've that meeting with the foreign minister in the city this morning anyway. You can't miss that."

"No," he pulled her to him anyway, pressing against her back, his hands smoothing over her stomach, and then further until she sucked in a sharp breath. "I can't miss that. I'll be back tonight. As soon as I can. And then we'll have to work out something a little more permanent."

She frowned, peeled off his hands and walked to the bathroom. "Tonight then." She closed the door and leaned against it for a moment. Something more permanent? What did he mean? What did he want? Come to that, she thought, as she began to shower, what did *she* want? She'd only ever wanted one thing—her estate, Senlisse. But now she couldn't have it. But she still couldn't imagine living anywhere else, not even in this dramatically beautiful country.

SHE SHOULD NEVER HAVE LET Sahmir kiss her after she'd emerged from the bathroom, she thought, as she looked around for the guards at the small compound that had grown up around the mine.

That had been the problem, she decided, as she closed the door and sighed. No guards—they'd already gone on to their next assignment. Her eyes alighted on a truck. No, she'd promised Sahmir she'd not go out alone. She went back into the building and sat at her desk and flicked open a few files and glanced at the diary. Damn. One of the engineers was flying back to Europe tomorrow and he wanted the samples analyzed before he left. What was she going to do? Sit here and twiddle her thumbs all because one man was being over-protective? Or risk it?

She glanced at her watch. If she didn't go now, it'd be too hot to go later. She wouldn't be long. All she had to get was a few soil samples so the scientists could complete their work today. If she delayed, the project would be delayed. Sahmir was being over-protective. Nothing would happen to her so far away from France. If the Russian was going to come after her, he'd have done so by now. And now, according to Sahmir's investigations, the Russian was embroiled in bigger affairs—some problem with rival gangs if the private investigator reports were accurate.

Besides, Sahmir would never know. She grinned and picked up the keys off the desk and strode out to the truck.

CHAPTER 10

Sahmir put down the phone and rubbed his lip thoughtfully. He got up from his desk and stretched. His over-used body reminded him of Rory. He half-groaned as he remembered making love to her. He couldn't get enough of her. But then his smile fell.

He'd lied to her.

Yes, he'd had a meeting with the foreign minister, but not Ma'in's. He'd just finished talking to the Foreign Minister of Roche, the Principality where Senlisse, Rory's estate, was. It wasn't the first of such conversations but it looked like being the last. Sahmir had finally persuaded him that the Roche government really didn't want the Russian mob to own a sizable estate within its borders. Advising the minister of some little-known facts about the *Solntsevskaya Bratva* had clinched the argument. The Minister had agreed to exploit any number of the loopholes that existed within its legal system to stop the Russian taking possession of the land.

He hadn't told Rory because he didn't want her returning to her beloved estate immediately. With the Russian seeing himself above the law, it still wasn't safe for her there. But he knew her, knew the pull she had to her land. And he also recognized, at an entirely selfish level, he didn't want her to go.

∼

It was pretty here, Rory thought, glancing up at the leaves that swayed in the light desert breeze. The only sounds were the rustling leaves and the water which ran over the stones on the river bed.

Pretty but kind of creepy. She quickly turned back to finish what she was doing, focusing on writing the labels on the bottles and putting them back into her bag, when she froze—her skin prickled all over and a trickle of sweat ran down her back.

She looked up. Standing before her were two men, their faces obscured by scarves and sunglasses. But what her eyes fixed on were the guns they were both carrying. Not slung over their shoulders, but held, aimed… at her.

"Hey! Who are you? What do you want?" Her voice was shaky, not as strong as she'd hoped it'd be.

A string of unknown words was issued. It sounded like a question. But not a friendly one. She hadn't a clue what they'd said but they hadn't advanced on her. She took a step backward, toward where the truck was parked. She shook her head. "I don't understand what you're saying."

They repeated the words. But before she could move, the larger man at the front stepped forward. He pushed her back with the front of his gun and peered at her face. She stumbled backwards. She held her arms out wide. "I have nothing here. No money, no drugs… nothing!"

He spoke again in a language she'd never heard before but she got the gist. He wasn't friendly. He wasn't looking at anywhere other than her. He prodded her again in the

CLAIMED BY THE SHEIKH

stomach with the gun and said something and looked around, as if he'd said something amusing. The other man laughed as the first man prodded her once more with the gun.

She stumbled back, and turned quickly, determined to make a dash for it, and found herself held by another man who'd come up from behind. He, too, was swathed in robes and scarves. Only the lower half of his face was visible and much of that was covered in a full beard.

"What do you want?"

"Want?" he repeated in heavily accented English. "You, of course." Then she felt the first man's filthy hand clamp a chemical smelling cloth over her face. She struggled, tried to lash out, while the men's grip tightened on her. Then, suddenly, all the energy seemed to sap out of her. The last thing she saw before she lost consciousness was one of the men, staring at her closely, his foul breath upon her face. Then all went black.

SAHMIR SWUNG AROUND, incredulous—fury and fear fighting for ascendancy. "You did what? What the hell were you thinking? You had strict instructions—"

"Do you know where she went?" interrupted Tariq, addressing the terrified guards.

"Yes, Your Royal Highness, we found the truck she used."

Sahmir paced from one side of the small room to another. "Nothing else? No clue?"

"Nothing. Except her bag of soil and water samples. Her purse wasn't there but the rest of what was left behind was definitely hers."

Sahmir slumped against the wall. "She wasn't robbed. She never carried money or credit cards—or a wallet for that matter. Money doesn't interest her and there's little use for it in the desert anyway. It wasn't money they were after. It was her."

"Have you had the Bedouin trackers take a look?" continued Tariq.

"Yes, Your Highness. They tracked horses back over the mountains to the border with Hadramout."

"Looks like they're headed for the port. They went the long way around, avoiding the border guards," said Sahmir. He closed his eyes, imagining the scene—his Rory, bound and slung over the back of a horse while unknown men took her further away from him.

"It would seem so, Your Highness."

Tariq picked up the phone. "I'll get our men onto it."

"And I'll alert Safiyeh," said Sahmir. "She'll help if she can. I'll do it on the way."

"On the way where?"

"To Hadramout, of course. We should intercept them on their way down into the port." Sahmir glanced at Aarif. "Get the chopper ready. We leave immediately."

Rory woke up and groaned. She tried to swallow but her mouth and throat were dry. She opened her eyes to find she was lying under a low overhanging rock. To one side of the overhang she could see a strip of dark blue—late evening sky, already pricked with stars. She tried to move her hands and feet but they were tied firmly and she winced as the movement caused the ropes to press deeper into her chafed flesh.

She lay still as she tried to assess her situation. She must have been knocked out for at least eight hours, possibly longer. She could hear voices a little way away and the crackle of a fire. She shifted her head to one side and inhaled the smell of roasted meat. Despite her queasiness, her stomach grumbled. Between two stumpy bushes, tall shadows moved around a fire. There looked to be just the three of them—presumably the same three who'd captured her. A shiver wracked her body and cold sweat bloomed on her forehead. She felt sick and chilled. What the hell had they drugged her with?

Was it just the three of them? Could she get away? She looked around. If she could stand up she might be able to shuffle somewhere. But where? She had no idea where she was and no idea in which direction to proceed. The ground she lay on was rocky, and they looked to be in the bottom of a 'V' of some kind of mountain pass. They must have climbed up into the mountains that marked the frontier between Hadramout and Ma'in.

She rolled on to her stomach and with difficulty pushed herself to standing. But suddenly there was a shout and the men were upon her.

"Stay!"

"Down!"

Two of the men shouted at her, as if she were a dog.

"No!" she croaked. "Water, give me water."

The man who'd come up behind her yesterday, whose English was better than the others, nodded to another who went back to the small camp and brought her a bottle of water.

"Where are you taking me?" She addressed the first man. He was obviously in charge.

He shrugged. "To the man who paid us to find you, of course." He grinned, a rotten-toothed grin. "There is nothing you can do, so sit ...drink."

The second man came up with the bottle. She indicated her hands but he shook his head. Instead he brought the bottle to her mouth, squirted it into her face and then into her mouth, laughing as she choked and gulped down the precious water.

She turned aside and coughed. The men turned away as if to resume their seats at the campfire. "Wait!" she spluttered between coughs. "Whatever this man is paying you, I promise you more."

They laughed. The boss looked at her, almost with pity. "There is no-one with enough money to make me cross this man."

"Yes there is! I can arrange it!"

But her words fell on deaf ears as they returned to their meal and their cigarettes.

She continued to stand for several minutes but she felt weak and exhausted and her ankles throbbed under their tight constraints. She suddenly realized it was a pointless waste of energy and sat back down again. She'd conserve her energy—that's what she'd do—and when it was totally dark and they were sleeping, she'd try to get away. She lay back down. Whatever they'd given her it was potent stuff. She felt totally exhausted. She'd close her eyes... just for a while... rest... then she'd escape.

She was awoken by the discomfort of the lumpy stones on which she lay. And the smell. Someone had dumped a disgusting blanket over her while she'd slept. She couldn't decide if the overriding smell was sweat or horse dung. Sweat, she eventually decided. It was too disgusting to be horse dung.

The fire had burned low but she could just make out the three sleeping forms, dark lumps against the light of the dying embers. She should make a move now, but when she tried to flex her swollen hands and feet, she knew she wasn't going anywhere. Instead she lay back and looked up at the stars that Sahmir had told her about only weeks before.

She gulped down a sob. They were the same stars, she told herself. Somewhere Sahmir was looking at them, wondering where she was. No, not wondering, she told herself sternly. He'd be following them. He'd be waiting until it was dark and then he'd make his move. Her eyes burned as she tried to keep them open, listening, watching, waiting for Sahmir to appear. He *would*. She knew he would. If she counted the stars, one by one, he'd arrive when she got to a hundred... five hundred...

She awoke with a start, heart thumping, eyes alert. She looked around the small clearing in which they'd set up camp and realized it was getting close to dawn. She also felt something... what she didn't know. But she felt impelled to sit up. Someone was near. She knew it. She could feel it. There was a tension in the air. It was darker than before, as the fire had gone out, but the drugs must have worn out of her system and she felt a prickle of awareness travel down her spine. She struggled to standing and then a hand came around her mouth. She tried to scream, but then he pulled her back against his chest and she smelled him, that wonderful smell that she could never get enough of.

She twisted her mouth to his face and breathed his name, "Sahmir..."

Even this close she couldn't see him properly but he placed his finger against her lips and she nodded in agreement. Quietly, so quietly, he picked her up and handed her to someone else who walked away from the scene and kept on walking. She wriggled in this man's arms. She knew he was one of Sahmir's men, but she didn't want to leave Sahmir. Once out of sight of the men he set her to her feet and cut through her bindings. She rubbed her wrists and flexed her feet. While the bodyguard's attention was distracted by the other men who also waited there for some kind of signal, she crept back so she could see what was going on.

The early morning grey light was beginning to filter into

the clearing and she could clearly see the men were massively outnumbered. It should have relieved her worry but instead she was frantic. Standing above the three men, alone, was Sahmir.

It all happened so quickly. Suddenly Sahmir grabbed the man who was the leader and pulled him to his feet. The man started babbling in his language and bowing, demonstrating his subservience now that he knew he was outnumbered, but Sahmir kept repeating the same words. She couldn't quite make them out. Whatever Sahmir was saying produced more incoherent babble from the man. She walked a little closer. And then she heard it for a third time.

"Did you touch her?"

This time the words were followed by a fist into the man's jaw. He went out cold. Sahmir turned to the other kidnappers, held by his men, and Rory could see he was about to ask the same question. She walked up behind him and placed a hand on his arm. Sahmir turned around and Rory almost stepped back under the blast of his furious gaze. But she didn't.

"Sahmir, it's me. And no, they didn't touch me. Just bound me. That's all. Sahmir?" Slowly the glazed anger in his eyes faded and Sahmir closed his eyes tight and then opened them again and drew her into his arms.

"What the hell were you thinking, Rory?" he asked angrily as he kissed the top of her head.

She couldn't have answered even if she'd wanted to—she was pressed so close against his chest.

"I told you never to go anywhere without your bodyguards but you didn't listen."

She was so tight against him that she could feel his heartbeat vibrate through her body—his blood pounding as if it were her own. "I'm sorry," she murmured. "Please…" She pressed the palms of her hands against his chest and tried to prize herself away. It took her far enough to see the fury had been replaced by tears. No, he wasn't angry any more, he was scared.

He kissed her again. "Don't do that again, Rory. You could have died."

"But I didn't. I didn't die, Sahmir."

Whether her words reassured him or not, she couldn't have said. He picked her up in his arms and carried her, her head and body held tightly against his, back down the track to where vehicles were now arriving to take them back to Ma'in.

She awoke to a soft light pressing against her closed lids. She opened her eyes to see the bright sunshine of the palace in Ma'in City filtered through drawn curtains. She sighed and stretched out her legs, circling her still sore ankles, and turned to see Sahmir sitting watching her. He rose and sat on the bed. "Good morning, sleepy head."

She grinned and stretched. "How long have I been asleep?"

"Long enough to have recovered from your ordeal, hopefully."

She yawned and felt very contented. "No really, how long?"

"About six hours. The after-effects of the drug they forced you to inhale, I believe."

She met his gaze and in that moment their fears were evident. "It was terrifying, Sahmir. I thought I'd never see you, or my family, again. I thought the Russian had got me this time. Because it *was* him who was behind it, wasn't it?"

Sahmir nodded in agreement. "It was."

"But why? I don't understand why he went to so much trouble, just for my signature." She looked across at Sahmir who was frowning, the expression in his eyes more serious than she'd ever seen before. "Sahmir? What is it? Is there something I don't know?"

He hesitated, then nodded once. "We interrogated the men who took you. They confirmed what I already knew. It wasn't just your signature he wanted. You remember the fight you witnessed? Where the Russian pulled a knife on someone? He *did* kill a man that night and you witnessed it. He wanted your signature first and then he was going to make sure you didn't say anything against him."

"How? How did he hope to do that?" She laughed uncomfortably.

But Sahmir wasn't laughing. "You really don't want to know, Rory."

She sat down, suddenly weak. "*Mon Dieu*! He was going to kill me."

"Possibly, or do something else extreme enough to stop you from talking. Whatever his plans, you can be sure they wouldn't be pleasant for you. I'm sorry, I should have told you before. I wanted to keep you safe and I wanted to keep you *feeling* safe."

"So I'm never going to be free of him?"

"Yes, you are. I've been playing by the rules up till now. Doing everything legally. But I know things the police will be interested to hear. I've been around, seen things they'll want to know about, things that should help get him out of our lives for good."

"But I can tell them what I've seen."

"No way. You keep out of this. I'll deal with it."

"But—"

"No, Rory. It's not your fight any more. It's between me and him." He kissed her gently on her lips. "Now go back to sleep, rest, get well. You're safe here and I'll make sure you're always safe."

CLAIMED BY THE SHEIKH

Despite his assurances, an uneasy sense of being smothered came over her. "And what are you going to do?"

He turned to her, the smiling, charming face of her Sahmir now gone completely. "I'm going to finish this business once and for all."

As the door clicked shut, Rory lay back on the bed. She had no choice, she still felt so weak. Despite the weakness there was a fluttering of fear inside and it wasn't only because of the Russian. She was scared *for* Sahmir. And she was also scared of being trapped in this beautiful palace by a man who was afraid to let her be free.

∼

SAHMIR'S SISTER'S VOICE—THE voice of compassion and reason—floated into his mind. She'd always told him to avoid trouble if at all possible. But then, if it came his way, to deal with it. Whatever was required to turn a wrong into a right—simply do it.

As a kid that had meant admitting it was he who'd thrown the cricket ball into the glasshouse and helping to clear it up, not leave it to the servants like others did.

Well, he wasn't in trouble but the woman he loved was, which was the same thing.

Ensiyeh, wherever you are, look away.

He turned back to the desk and flicked through his phone contacts. He'd moved in the Russian's circles for years. He knew things that the Russian's many enemies would be very interested to hear.

Time to play dirty.

Whatever it takes, Ensiyeh, to turn a wrong into a right.

SAHMIR FINISHED his phone call just as Tariq entered the

room. But he didn't turn around. Instead he poured himself a stiff whiskey. "Want one?" he asked Tariq.

"Are you celebrating or drowning your sorrows?"

Sahmir didn't answer immediately. Instead he took a mouthful of whiskey and waited for the alcohol to enter his blood stream. "I'm not drowning my sorrows."

"But you're not celebrating either?"

Sahmir shook his head. He'd avoided doing what he'd just done for a long time, knowing the potential chaos it could cause both personally and politically. But he'd been forced into it.

"Sahmir, what have you done?"

He inhaled a steadying breath. "What I had to do."

"I hope you haven't jeopardized the security of Ma'in in protecting Rory?"

Sahmir glanced at his eldest brother for the first time since he'd entered the room. Tariq stood with arms crossed and brow lowered. Sahmir knew that stance. Tariq had no intention of leaving Sahmir's office until he knew what Sahmir had done.

He sighed and walked over to the window. The sun was about to rise. He'd been up all night talking with the right people... and the wrong people, until he'd accomplished his goal.

"This has nothing to do with Ma'in; it can't be traced to me. I've relayed information the French Police would be interested in learning about Vadim. Damning information about the death of a fellow Russian. Information that will get him locked away."

Tariq narrowed his eyes. "And how successful are the Police going to be at prosecuting Vadim?"

Sahmir smiled. "Not very. That's why I made sure a certain member of the Police—very senior—would be told."

"Because?"

Sahmir turned to face Tariq then, his gaze steady. He wanted to see how Tariq took what he was about to tell him. "Because he's in the pay of a rival gang to Vadim's."

Tariq nodded slowly. "And the murdered man... I'm guessing he was a member of this rival gang?"

Sahmir nodded.

"You're leaving it to the rival gang to mete out justice to Vadim."

Again Sahmir nodded.

"That's dangerous stuff. You've chosen to destabilize the Russian mafia to protect Rory."

"You're suggesting Vadim's gang was ever stable?"

"You know exactly what I mean."

"I do. And I had no choice. It's done."

"So... what now?"

"We wait. It shouldn't take long. Timing is everything to these people. I've planted a ticking bomb. It won't take long to explode."

"Does Rory know?"

"No. There's no need for her to know the details."

"Because then she'll know how just how far back you and Vadim go."

Sahmir winced. He hated to be reminded of that dark time. Not that he'd been implicated in any crime, but just being on the fringes of the Russian's world had been enough to sicken him. And would surely be enough to sicken her. "I'd rather she didn't know that. And she doesn't need to."

"Fine by me."

Sahmir finished the last of his whiskey and walked back to the desk, picked up his phone and slipped it into his pocket. "I'm going to see Rory now. I'll let you know when there's any news."

"'When', not 'if?'"

"Oh yes, Tariq. Vadim is living on borrowed time."

Tariq shook his head grimly and Sahmir walked out of the office. He felt sick to his stomach. He felt as bad as the Russian and his mob. But there'd been no other way. As long as Vadim lived, Rory would never be safe. He walked slowly up the stairs, paused at Rory's room, and then continued to his own. He couldn't face anyone—not even Rory—yet.

Instead, he lifted the photograph of his sister from his bureau, remembering snippets of the lectures she'd used to give him. Avoid trouble. At all costs avoid trouble. And then the part that he'd held in his mind for the past twenty-four hours. But if trouble comes your way, deal with it—decisively and effectively.

Ensiyeh, my beautiful sister, you'd be proud.

But even as he whispered the words, in his heart he doubted it.

~

Rory lay on her side on the bed, looking out at the flowers that framed the window, bright in the early morning sun, wondering what was going on with Sahmir. Ever since they'd returned from the desert he'd been tense. Even during the night he couldn't keep still and had ended up disappearing for most of the night.

A knock at the door roused her from her thoughts.

"Come in!"

Sahmir entered and walked up to the end of the bed, not coming to her as he usually did, not greeting her with a smile and compliment, but just standing there, his expression serious.

She sat up immediately. "Sahmir, what is it? You've been behaving so strangely. You must tell me."

"The Russian—Vadim—he's dead. There's been a big mafia bust-up in Europe with deaths on both sides."

"Dead?" Rory gulped. "Dead? I don't believe it? How?"

"Seems his rival gang got to hear of some atrocities he committed on some of their members. They retaliated."

"But how did they get to hear..." Her voice trailed off as she looked up at him. Something wasn't right.

"Vadim's dead," he said, not answering her question. "That's all that's important. You're safe now."

She sat back on her pillows, shocked. "*Dieu merci*! I can't believe it! I'm free of him. I can return to Europe, see my family again." Then she frowned. "But where does that leave the estate? Senlisse?"

He came over and sat beside her, and took her hand in his. "With you. My lawyers have been working with your government, who weren't best pleased to discover a member of the *Solntsevskaya Bratva* had now claimed one of their oldest estates. They'll be more than happy to reinstate you and your family as owner."

"Are you sure?"

"I'm sure. That's what they told me."

"You *have* been busy." Then she looked at him again and frowned. There was something more. She could see it in Sahmir's eyes. This was the best news for them both and yet... somehow it was all too neat. Too soon after her kidnapping. Something was wrong. Somehow Sahmir was implicated. He had to be. "How did you do it, Sahmir?"

He pulled away from her. "I told you, my solicitors."

"You know what I mean."

At that moment there was a knock at the door and Sahmir, obviously glad of the interruption, opened it, had a brief exchange with someone and then returned with a pile of newspapers.

"What is it? Something to do with the Russian?"

He frowned. "I don't know. Something Aarif apparently thinks I should see straight away."

She rose out of bed, pulled on a dressing gown and walked up beside him as he spread out one of the papers on the table. As soon as he opened it out, she saw the photo. He tried to close it but her hand held it firmly in place.

The surge of emotion she felt when she saw who the picture was of, was nearly overwhelming. Although the photograph was grainy and over-enlarged, there was no doubt that at its center, around the table with a few other men, was her father. She gasped. "It's Papa!"

The tears sprang to her eyes and she took the paper and walked over to the window seat in an effort to have some privacy. She pushed the side of her hand heavily against her forehead, sheltering her eyes as she tried to hold back the tears, but they came anyway.

She held the paper in shaking hands, feasting on the image of her father. So intent was she on staring at his beloved face that it took her a few minutes for her eyes to stray to the men seated around him. The photograph was obviously a snap, taken surreptitiously with no thought given to focus or light or the subjects posing. No-one was smiling. Her father was frowning uncharacteristically, his face slightly blurred as if he'd been called to turn around a second before some unknown person had taken the photograph.

Then she saw him. The Russian, facing the camera, head on, with a smug expression on his face as if he knew the photograph was being taken. As if he'd arranged it for his own devious purposes. She gasped. "It's him." She was about to put it away when she looked at the person seated to the other side of the Russian. It was Sahmir. She gasped, and dropped the paper.

He picked it up. Looked at it for a long time, his expression unchanging and then looked up at her, with eyes she'd not seen before. They were hard. Fear ripped through her.

"Sahmir..." Her voice was hoarse, the word only a whisper. "What..." She couldn't get any more words out.

"What am I doing here?" He glanced back at the photograph. "I'm playing Blackjack with the Russian and your father. I'd forgotten about Vadim's predilection for having inappropriate photos taken. Always useful for blackmail."

"You—" She licked her lips and swallowed, her mouth suddenly too dry to speak. "You knew my father."

"Yes. And it looks like Vadim wanted to make sure you knew." He tossed the paper down. "Not knowing that it'd be one of his last acts before he was killed." He turned back to face Rory. "Yes, I knew your father."

"You played cards with my father."

He sighed heavily. "I didn't know he was your father at first. But yes. I played Blackjack with him."

"You played cards with him," she repeated, desperately trying to understand. She glanced at the paper again. "You're sitting next to him. You knew him. And yet you said nothing to me." She looked into Sahmir's eyes, wanting to obliterate the doubts that filled her mind. "Why didn't you tell me?"

"That first night? I didn't know you were related." He shook his head. "And afterwards? What was the point? I didn't want to upset you."

"You didn't want to upset me?"

He ran his hands up her arms, holding her in place. She threw them off and backed away. "Rory, don't do this. It's not as it seems."

"It *seems*, that you knew my father, you played cards with him, you probably beat him. How much did you win? Is that why you didn't tell me? How much money did my father lose to you over the years? Did you work with the Russian?" She turned away, pushing her hair back off her face as she tried to process these new facts about Sahmir. "I've been so stupid. You knew the Russian because you'd played with him and my father. Were you there when my father lost the estate? With a different hand would you have won the estate, rather than the Russian? You ruined him between you."

"No! It wasn't like that."

She jumped up. "Then what the hell was it like?" She took the paper from him and twisted it around, holding the picture in front of his face. "My *father*. His *life*. My *estate*. All destroyed. And you knew all about it. You were probably there at the time. And yet you said nothing to me. You're as bad as the Russian."

"No." He grabbed hold of her. "No! Listen to me, Rory. It didn't happen like that."

"Then tell me how it *did* happen."

"Yes, I knew your father. Years ago, when I was gambling heavily, I knew him. Then I stopped and he didn't." He sighed. "A few weeks ago I went back to it again. I was there, that night that he must have lost Senlisse, but I left the game early. I'd done what I needed to do to get the funds Ma'in needed."

"I thought you'd raised them through a French investment company?"

"I did. And I topped it up at the gaming tables."

"You risked the money you raised?"

"No. I knew I wouldn't lose it. What I risked was my sanity. You see, I turned my back on that lifestyle years ago. But I've changed. I got what I wanted out of it and then I was about to leave Paris when you showed up."

Suddenly all the fight went out of her and she slumped onto the chair. "Why didn't you stop the game?"

"I tried. But your father was intent on continuing. There was nothing I could do to help. He was in too deep with the wrong people. I'd seen people like him before. Just one more game and then everything would be well. Just one more throw of the dice, one more deal."

"There was nothing you could do, so you left?" She closed her eyes briefly, trying to contain the anger she felt for not just Sahmir, but her father too.

"You think I didn't speak to him, you think I didn't try? Of *course* I did. He heard me out, told me it was too late for him and turned and went straight back in. I couldn't stay."

"No, you couldn't stay. And that was why you helped me. Not just kindness. But *guilt*."

She held up her hand to stop Sahmir from saying anything further. She couldn't bear hearing about the last few hours of her father's life—how helpless he'd been.

"You fooled me, Sahmir. I thought you were different to the Russian when in fact you were his friend, you were the same as him."

"Rory, I've never professed to be perfect. I've made mistakes, I've done things I regret, but *not* this. I had nothing to do with your father losing Senlisse."

"Maybe not, but you were a part of that world that I hate. And somehow you're implicated in the Russian's death. Aren't you?"

Sahmir didn't speak.

She stepped away again, appalled at all she didn't know about Sahmir—her trust in him shaken. She turned away and thrust her fingers through her hair, gripping her head.

"Let me explain, Rory."

"No."

He didn't move. "You won't listen to anything I have to say?" Sahmir reached out for her, but she threw him off and looked around.

She suddenly felt panicky, caged. "I need to get out of here."

He placed his hand on her arm and his fingers curled around her, too tightly. "Don't go like this. Let's talk it through."

She shook her head. "There's nothing more to say. Let me go."

The silence lengthened and slowly he loosened his grip on her arm.

She took a deep, sharp breath, not looking into his eyes. She shook her head. "I could never have imagined... I never thought..."

"Let me explain."

She looked up into his eyes then. "What's the point? Bottom line? You're as bad as all the rest of them."

Was he as bad as the Russian? Sahmir sank back against the wall as that word—guilt—slammed back into his mind and stayed there, as he examined it from all angles. Was she correct? Was it a feeling of guilt because he hadn't tried hard enough to save her father from losing everything, including himself, that had made him want to save Rory?

Sahmir leaned back against the wall and watched as she picked up the phone and asked for a seat on the next flight out of Ma'in. She was so desperate to leave him that she didn't even mind where the flight was going to. She'd get to France, and then to Roche, eventually. More to the point, she'd get away from him immediately.

Was she right? Was it guilt? Maybe a little, but not entirely. Whose actions were ever motivated by one thing? He'd done it because he needed to, and he couldn't separate out his pure instincts from those molded by heartache and experience. They became one. He waited until she finished another call—this time to his driver.

"You're wrong, Rory. When I first saw you I had no idea who you were, or who you were involved with. I ran after you, I wanted to help you, not from any sense of guilt, but from pure instinct."

The anger in her eyes faltered for a moment, revealing a hurt that he felt deep inside.

"That might be true, I don't know what to believe any more. But later you must have found out. And you came back for me." She moved around, picking up her things, throwing them into a suitcase. "I have to go. I have to get out of here."

"What about your work?"

"They can continue without me now."

He put his hand on her arm. "Don't leave like this, Rory."

He felt the energy slip out of her. "Sahmir." Her voice was barely a whisper. She turned to him and the sadness and disillusionment in her eyes nearly undid him. "How do you want me to leave? To say polite things like 'Thanks for saving my life, but I have to go now?' Or maybe you want us to make love one more time? Hey?" She shook her head. "It doesn't work like that. You left my father alone, with that, that *man* who finished him off. Finished *us* off," she added quietly.

Sahmir bit his tongue. He couldn't tell her the truth—the truth that her father had finished himself off. Nothing could have stopped him from self-destructing.

"You're going back to France?"

"Yes."

There was a knock at the door. Sahmir went and opened it. A nervous looking driver stood outside.

"Apologies, Miss Aurora asked me to come as soon as possible."

Sahmir summoned up a version of his usual polite self. "She'll be with you soon. Go, wait in the car." He closed the door. "At least let me take you."

"No, Sahmir. I need to get out. Now. Please, let me go."

"Only if you promise to call me if you need anything. Anything at all. Promise me."

She shook her head. "I can't promise anything. I can

hardly think straight, I'm so confused, Sahmir. I thought I knew you. But I don't know you at all and that scares me." She picked up her bags. "I want to leave."

With all his heart he wanted to hold her, keep her there, make her listen to reason. But he'd never kept anything or anyone against their will and he never would. He stepped aside.

She opened the door and walked outside into the corridor. She stopped at the end and turned, pausing. For one brief moment he thought she'd reconsidered, for one brief moment there seemed a possibility that their eyes could communicate more effectively than any words. And then she turned and walked away. And the moment was gone.

CHAPTER 11

Three months later...

Sahmir sat back wearily in his seat and nudged Daidan's foot with his own. Daidan, looking less weary, but equally ill at ease, stopped drumming his fingers on the fine linen tablecloth and turned to Sahmir, with an arrogantly raised brow. "Do you really have to resort to attracting my attention as if you were sixteen years old?"

Sahmir sighed. "Yes." He took a sip of his champagne and leaned on the table, indicating the happy couple with his wine glass who sat further along. "Look at them. I've never seen Tariq so happy. He can't take his eyes off Cara."

A glimmer of a smile passed over Daidan's face. The first Sahmir had seen since he'd arrived back in Ma'in for the wedding. "She's a lovely woman. Perfect for Tariq."

"Yes, I know. Pretty good judgement on my part."

Daidan glanced at Sahmir, patently unimpressed with his younger brother. "You set them up based on her voice. I hardly think you can claim any credit."

Sahmir frowned, indignant. "Yes I can. All it took was her

voiceover for that chocolate ad, and I knew she'd be right for Tariq. That required a certain amount of skill."

Daidan snorted. "What you imagined was a sultry woman with loose morals who'd give Tariq some entertainment for a week."

"Yes, well, I might have got the details wrong, but I'd got the big picture right. They're in it for the long haul. Together forever... and"— he waved his champagne glass in the air —"all that stuff."

Daidan frowned. "It's not like you to sound so offhand and cynical about love. I thought you were something of an expert."

"Huh," Sahmir snorted derisively. He drank some more. "I'm about as good as you."

It was Daidan's turn to drink. "That bad?"

Sahmir nodded slowly. "Oh, yes."

They both drank quietly for a few moments. "What happened to that woman, Aurora, who came here a few months ago?"

Sahmir put down his drink and sighed. "How did you hear about her?"

"Tariq wanted to know if I knew anything about her. He said you'd really fallen for her."

"He was wrong. Why would I fall for someone who has no interest in me?"

"It's not logical but then love isn't, is it?"

For the first time in a long time, Sahmir wondered if Daidan missed his wife who'd left him on their wedding day and never returned. "Did you love Taina?"

Daidan's expression didn't change. "Yes."

"Do you still?"

Daidan didn't miss a beat. "Yes. But it makes no difference."

Sahmir looked back at Tariq and Cara, talking quietly

together, with no eyes for anyone but each other. He was shocked by Daidan's admission. Daidan was always so strong, so unexpressive that he'd wrongly assumed he wasn't touched by the things that had happened to him. "You're right. It doesn't."

"I made a mistake a year ago," Daidan continued in the same strong, certain voice, devoid of emotion.

"What was that?"

For the first time, Daidan turned and looked at Sahmir, his eyes catching Sahmir's and holding them there by sheer force of character. "I should have followed her. I *should* have made things right between us."

"But surely you can still go after her? Do you know where she is?"

Daidan sat back in his chair. "Yes. The credit card receipts leave a trail from one glamorous resort to another. One month New York, and then Aspen, Dubai, the Maldives."

"You still pay her bills?"

"Of course. After all she still has shares in the company."

"Then why don't you go after her?"

"It's too late for me. But it's not for you. If you really like this woman, then go to her, tell her, make her see how you feel, and don't leave until she understands."

Sahmir began to shake his head but Daidan gripped his shoulder fiercely. "Just do it, Sahmir. Don't fuck up like I did."

Sahmir was stunned both by his brother's language—Daidan never swore—and his meaning. "She made it clear when she left that she didn't want anything to do with me."

"Do you know where she is?"

"Yes. She's back living on her estate with her mother and sister. I made enquiries. I needed to know she was okay but that's it. She's not interested—she was quite clear about that.

"People say all kinds of things in the heat of the moment. Ignore it, go find her."

"No, I can't do that."

"Yes, you can." Daidan sat back in his chair. "Go to France and claim her."

"*Claim* her! What do you think I am?"

"A man in love. This is no time for indecision."

"You're right, it's not. And I've decided to leave it to her. She knows the truth about me and my past, and if she wants to return to me she can."

Daidan shrugged. "It's up to you."

Sahmir sat back in his chair. "Yes, it is. Rory is the bird who's healed and flown away."

Daidan frowned. "What the hell are you talking about?"

"When I was a child…" Sahmir began. Then he shook his head. "Never mind. What I'm trying to say is you can't claim a living creature, a free creature."

No further enlightened, Daidan rose. "I've no idea what the hell you're talking about so I'm leaving." He glanced at Tariq and Cara who only had eyes for each other. "Somehow I don't think I'll be missed."

Sahmir followed Daidan's gaze and quickly turned away, pained by the sight of a love that he'd never now experience.

"Think I'll call it a night too."

With a heavy heart he followed Daidan down the empty corridors.

~

Senlisse, Roche

Rory stabbed the garden fork into the weed-free kitchen garden and straightened her back.

She breathed deeply of the crisp spring air and thanked

the Lord that her spell of morning sickness had been brief. Or maybe it had disappeared simply because she, her mother and her sister were all happily settled back at Senlisse.

Her mother said that was a ridiculous notion. Morning sickness was morning sickness and there was nothing to be done but endure it.

Rory wasn't so sure. She'd felt different since she'd been back here. They'd waited a month or so at St Malo until they'd returned, just to make sure there were no repercussions. But they needn't have worried. It seemed the Russian mob were more interested in regrouping on their own territory than concerning themselves with battling a foreign power with a dubious claim to an ancient Roche estate.

She looked around the sunlit garden, appreciating it all anew. From the orchard trees, now in full blossom, to the dappled sunlight warm on the brick walls of the kitchen garden, and the pungent aromas of lavender and thyme that filled the air. She loved it, felt at peace here and yet… something was missing. No, she was wrong. Some *one* was missing.

She reached into her old gardening jacket, pulled out the well-thumbed invitation she'd received some weeks ago and re-read it, her fingers tracing over the embossed lettering and the handwritten postscript, as if she'd feel something of the person whose signature it was.

"Rory!"

She looked up and waved to her sister, Marie-Laure, who was walking up the path from the chateau to the walled gardens where Rory was working. Rory slipped the invitation into her pocket.

"Maman said you shouldn't exert yourself so much, in your condition."

"Maman worries too much. Besides the fresh air makes me feel less queasy."

Marie-Laure narrowed her gaze and studied Rory's face. "Seriously, how *are* you feeling?"

Rory pulled a face. "I haven't vomited this morning, so that's good."

"Good." Marie-Laure frowned. "Then why are you as pale as a sheet?" She looped her arm through Rory's. "You can tell me while we walk back to the chateau. Maman has coffee and cake waiting."

As they walked back toward the chateau, Rory pulled out the invitation and handed it to her sister. Her sister read it and gave a low whistle and handed it back. "So what are you waiting for? It's about time you went to see Sahmir and told him he's going to be a father."

"Yes, I know. I *will* go. I'm just not sure when." She tapped the invitation on the palm of her hand.

"I don't know why you haven't gone before. You're obviously missing him."

"Maybe, but I haven't heard a thing from Sahmir… until this."

"I don't know why you're surprised after what you told him."

"Yes, I know. I just thought…" She sighed.

"Anyway, that note—I assume it's from him—'please come'. Simple, but direct. I like it."

Rory nodded.

"And so do you by the soft look on your face."

"Yes, but all that stuff with Papa… and Sahmir's involvement with the Russian… it just floored me."

"Rory! He got rid of the Russian, didn't he? We're back in our home because of Sahmir, aren't we? Come on, Rory, the Russian was a bad guy. He deserved everything he had coming to him."

Rory shook her head at her beautiful blonde sister.

"Didn't Maman ever tell you that 'two wrongs don't make a right?'"

"Yes. She also told me that we should be content with what we have. I never believed that either."

Rory's mouth dropped open as she watched her petite sister smile and open the door and greet their mother. She was so dainty, so angelic, and yet apparently had as black and white a view on life as Sahmir had.

Rory sat at the scrubbed oak kitchen table by the open French windows, while Marie-Laure walked across the stone-flagged kitchen—built on a scale for servants and cooking which was no longer required—and poured three cups of coffee. She placed two on the table and walked away with her own. "Maman! Tell Rory she should go to the opening of the reservoir in Ma'in. She's received an invitation but she's unsure whether to go. I'll leave you to it. All this indecision is driving me crazy." With that, Marie-Laure left the room.

Rory's mother glanced nervously at her eldest daughter and came and sat opposite Rory.

"So." She smiled uncertainly. "You can't decide whether to go to Ma'in, to see Sahmir?"

"I still feel angry Maman… with Sahmir… with Papa."

"Let it go, Rory. There's no point in holding on to it. There's more than yourself to consider now."

"I don't need a father for my baby!"

Her mother shook her head and sighed. "You always were headstrong. You inherited that from your father, luckily not the other thing."

"Why do you call Papa's gambling addiction a 'thing'? Why didn't we ever call things by their real names in our family?"

Her mother fidgeted with the pearls she still always wore around her neck. Just as she had every day at Senlisse where she'd worked from sunrise to sunset to keep the chateau looking like it had when she'd first married and they'd had servants. "Because our family didn't do things like that."

"Didn't speak the truth you mean?"

Her mother looked her sharply. "We didn't drag things into the mud, didn't destroy things if it wasn't necessary to do so."

Rory jumped up from the table and paced the kitchen floor. "*Maman*, I don't want things destroyed. I simply want to *know*, to *understand* about Papa. It would have made everything easier."

"Maybe for you. But while he was alive, it wouldn't have made things easier for him. You adored your father, and he adored you. You two always had such a special bond. How could I destroy the image you had of him?"

"It was the *wrong* image, *Maman*. The *wrong* image."

"Not entirely."

Her mother looked away, the grief on her face still fresh, and Rory felt a pang of guilt. "I'm sorry, Maman, but—"

The older woman raised her hand to stop Rory from speaking. "Albert was a good man, a loving man in many ways. He had just one problem."

"A major problem."

"Yes, of course it was major. It destroyed him. But after he died, what was the point of telling you, of explaining everything to you?"

"Because I would have understood what happened. And, if you'd told me earlier we could have got him help."

"No-one could have saved him, Aurora. Not even you."

"Not even me," Rory repeated softly. She shook her head and sat down again. "Maybe you're right. Maybe I couldn't have helped him. But knowing what was going on, at least I wouldn't have blamed other people."

"Aurora? What do you mean? Who else did you blame?"

"I saw in the papers a photograph of Papa, with the Russian, Vadim, and Sahmir. I thought…"

"Ah, I see. You thought Sahmir was to blame. Sahmir, who rescued you from the clutches of that dreadful Russian. *That* Sahmir."

"*That* Sahmir," she repeated, even though she couldn't imagine there being more than one Sahmir in the entire world.

"The Sahmir who's made sure we're safe and our future here at Senlisse is safe."

Rory fell back against the chair, feeling suddenly drained. "Yes, *that* Sahmir! Oh, Maman! What have I done?"

Her mother leaned over and pushed Rory's hair back from her face. "I don't know, Rory. But it's never too late to put things right. Go to Ma'in, attend the opening of the reservoir, tell Sahmir about the baby and… just see what happens."

"I think it's too late. Sahmir hates me. I rejected him, told him I never wanted to see him again. He's probably moved on by now. Found someone else."

"Of course. And that's why he's written you a note asking you to 'please come' to the opening."

Rory shrugged. "He's probably just being polite."

"Go!"

"How can I? I have no money, I'm lucky if I can last a day without vomiting and the father of my child probably hates me. He's probably engaged to some foreign princess by now." She bit her lip but a tear managed to escape and trickle down her cheek. Rory looked up at her mother, embarrassed.

But instead of sympathy her mother stood up and placed her hands on her tweed skirted hips. "Aurora Lucienne de Chambéry! This is *not* like you. This is your pregnancy hormones talking. Now, where's my practical, go-getting daughter gone? Hey? Deal with this, just as you have everything else."

"How?"

"Begin with a decision. After that everything else will be easy. Firstly decide to let your anger go. Sahmir *isn't* like your Papa. He moved in the same world as him for a while but he's stronger, he survived and moved on, unlike your Papa. Sahmir did what he had to do to sort out a bad situation decisively. There could have been no better outcome for us. And that's all thanks to Sahmir."

Rory nodded.

"And forget about your beloved Senlisse," continued her mother. "It's a place. Which would you rather have? A man who you love and who loves you, or Senlisse?"

Rory didn't hesitate. "Sahmir."

Her mother lifted her chin and smiled broadly. "It wasn't such a difficult decision, was it?"

Rory shook her head as she twisted the tissues between her fingers. "But how can I convince him that I love him?"

"Well, my darling girl, I'll leave that up to you. But one thing's for sure, you won't be able to do it from here."

Rory nodded. "You're right, as always." She rose and walked toward the hallway.

"And, Aurora?"

"Yes, Maman?"

"Don't go in those tatty jeans."

For the first time Rory smiled, both at her mother's refusal to lessen her standards, or those of her daughter, and at a thought that crept into her head.

"I promise I'll find something more suitable."

"Good. Now, go. Pack. I'll sort out a flight for you."

Rory smiled at her mother as she wiped the last of her tears away, strengthened by a ridiculous notion that refused to leave her as she climbed the grand staircase to her bedroom. She opened her wardrobe, plucked out some summer clothes and then her hand strayed to the red evening dress she'd worn the first night she'd met Sahmir. She pulled it out and held it up to the bright northern light that streamed in through the window.

She remembered what he'd said.

"Maybe one day we'll meet under different circumstances. And you'll wear that beautiful dress in the sunshine when you're happy."

It had been his way of saying he'd like to see her happy, out of the predicament she'd found herself in. Instead she'd made things worse and worse. Until now. Now she had to face up to it and put things right.

She'd show him the dress in the sunshine.

∽

A week later, Ma'in...

EVERYONE WAS at Jabal al Noor, the old Gold Mine 1 as its previous owners had called it, to see the water redirected from the new riverbed specifically manufactured to take it away from the site of the gold mine, back to its original wadi. The moment when the river would change course, and would spill into the old wadi and down into the depths of the mine, drowning out its old past and creating a new landscape with new opportunities, had been eagerly anticipated by the whole nation. It was only the beginning, there was still a lot to do, but it marked a turning-point in the country's history.

Sahmir stood beside Tariq and Cara, in front of the crowds and world media, listening with admiration to his eldest brother as he gave an opening speech full of passion and eloquence. Sahmir glanced at Cara, knowing that she was largely responsible for allowing the world to see the passionate man beneath the stern exterior. He caught her eye and they exchanged knowing smiles.

Then he looked around at the people who'd worked alongside Rory as they'd planned for this moment, when a new chapter of Ma'in would begin, and once more he felt the pain of her absence.

She wasn't here. She'd been invited but no response had been received. He wasn't surprised. Only disappointed. She'd made it quite clear what she'd wanted. And it wasn't him.

Suddenly it was Sahmir's turn to say a few words. He'd used to shun this side of political life but now he'd stepped forward. He'd do whatever was required to support his brother and his family. He no longer needed his sister's wise words to keep him on track. Tariq and he had discussed long into the night the future of the country and their respective roles. Tariq had surprised Sahmir by refusing his first suggestion of living full-time in Ma'in. Instead Tariq had suggested a compromise: Sahmir would be in charge of international business and diplomacy and live six months in Europe and six months in Ma'in. Sahmir had been intent on doing the right thing but when Tariq had suggested this, he'd quickly accepted. It was the perfect compromise. And Sahmir couldn't help but think that he may have the opportunity to see Rory again. He'd never force her to do anything. You didn't do that to people you loved. But persuasion was his strong suit, after all.

And, as he stepped up to the podium and twisted the microphone into position, he was aware it was his job to persuade the international community that Ma'in was a stable, prosperous country, that was open for business… with the right partners.

He narrowed his eyes against the glare. He smiled at the waiting crowds and then began to speak. He knew how to entertain, and soon had them in the palm of his hands.

And then it was over. The water began flowing back, covering the mine, masking the ugliness as if it had never existed. He wanted to go, retreat back to the desert castle, leave the celebrations to all the people who'd benefited from Rory's vision. Despite everything, he wasn't in the mood to celebrate.

He left as quickly as he could and was soon at Qusayr Zarqa, which was practically deserted for the day. He walked through the empty castle, remembering his time there with Rory. What was she doing now? At Senlisse, no doubt, planning her future and that of her beloved estate. There was no room in her life for anything or anyone else. She'd made that quite clear. He closed his eyes as a corroding combination of frustration and regret flooded his veins.

He looked around, suddenly feeling caged by the ancient walls, and walked outside, instinct taking him through the wild pistachio trees, down to the wadi, where he used to gain such comfort as a child.

HE WASN'T HERE EITHER! Rory had not only been too late for the ceremony, she was too late to catch Sahmir at Qusayr Zarqa. He must have returned to the city instead. The few staff who were there didn't seem able to tell her.

She returned to the Land Rover, tossed in her bag and was about to start up the engine, when she paused. Cara had told Rory that Sahmir had left early and that he'd been quiet.

Rory knew what that meant. She also remembered Sahmir telling her where he liked to go when he wanted to be on his own. She jumped out of the Land Rover once more and walked over to the wadi where the wild pistachio trees grew.

Sahmir couldn't have said what made him look up. There was no sound other than the flowing of the water over the stony river bed. Nothing other than the faint rustle of leaves high overhead, catching the breeze. But his skin prickled as if he were being watched. He looked up, his eyes scanning the shadowy trees.

Then he saw it. A flash of red weaving its way down the path toward him. He stood up, hardly daring to believe what he saw as the red took the form of a skirt, a skirt he remembered. And then the form emerged, running into the dappled sunlight—red skirt and scarves full and flowing, incongruous.

Was he imagining things? Was his mind, full of regrets, playing tricks on him?

"Rory?" he half-whispered.

Then she turned, saw him and her face broke into a big sunny smile. He still couldn't believe it was her and he shook his head in disbelief.

Her smile faded into uncertainty as she stepped forward out of the shelter of the trees. It *was* her, dressed in the full red-skirted evening dress, except this time, she'd added a red scarf which she'd wrapped around her head and body, hiding the black bodice and wonderful cleavage he knew lay beneath. "Rory?" he asked again, stronger now.

"So… you still remember my name then."

He walked toward her, unable to stop himself even if he'd wanted to. He wanted to pull her into his arms but couldn't. Not yet. Not until he knew the reason for her appearance.

"What are you doing here?"

"I came for the opening of the reservoir. I *was* invited, you know."

"I *do* know. But you didn't respond."

"No, I'm sorry. But I came anyway. Unfortunately I was too late, so I came looking for you."

"Why?"

She hesitated, as if suddenly unsure. He couldn't stand to see her unsure.

He took another step closer. "It's good to see you." His eyes hungrily sought her hair, her eyes, her cheeks and settled briefly on her lips before looking back into her eyes—blue eyes, the color of a northern sea—eyes, that suddenly flared with hope. He'd remembered the shape and form of her features, but how could he have forgotten how they made him feel? How *dear* they'd become to him. And yet... there was something different about her.

"Good to see you, too." She pressed her lips together and looked down. "More than good."

He waited for her to continue but neither moved, or spoke for long seconds. "Tell me why you came. Is it connected with the work you did on the mine? Did you really come back just for the opening?"

She looked up then and shook her head. "I came to tell you something." Again she hesitated, as if unsure how to proceed.

"Anything in particular?"

She nodded and stepped closer to him. Then she took hold of his hand and he melted. He tried to bring their joined hands up to his lips but she held on to him tightly—her eyes holding his with an urgency he couldn't refuse—forcing his hand to go another way... a different way... down to her stomach. He closed his eyes in an attempt to stem his feelings. Instead he felt more as his fingers fanned over her stomach. A stomach that his body remembered well. It had been flat. Now it wasn't.

He felt it viscerally—a leap of pure joy—before he could form the words. "You're pregnant," he whispered. It was neither a question nor a statement.

"I have your baby inside me, Sahmir."

His hand continued to explore her stomach while he tilted her face to face him. "Why didn't you tell me?"

"Because I wasn't sure you'd want to know. I wasn't sure…"

"What you wanted to do about it?"

She bit her lip and nodded.

"But you're here, now. Does that mean you know now?"

She nodded again.

"Then you need to tell me, and quickly before I go out of my mind."

"I can't stay in Senlisse on my own any more."

"Why? Is there a problem?"

She sighed. "A huge one. An insurmountable one. Sahmir, I'd willingly risk losing Senlisse, my sanity, anything to have you with me again. To have you touch me, to have you hold me in your arms again."

He exhaled heavily with relief. "Lucky for you then"—he reached out and swept his finger down her cheek—"that you won't have to lose your sanity for me to touch you." She closed her eyes and turned her lips to his touch. "Or to hold you… and our baby." He put his arms around her and brought her to him, pulling down her scarf as he did so, revealing the black bodice, trimmed with red lace.

He held her close and she melted into his arms. "Or to keep you here," he murmured as he kissed the top of her head. She looked up at him and they kissed, a sweet kiss full of tenderness.

When they pulled apart, Rory's lips quirked into a playful smile. "And how do you propose to keep me here, my Prince? By the power of your kiss, or the strength of your embrace alone?"

"I don't need to use my strength."

The smile flickered on her lips, lips that had featured in his dreams every night since she'd left.

"Is that right?" she breathed against his cheek.

He touched her chin gently—she'd hardly have felt it—yet she still raised her face to his. "By claiming you for my own, once and for all. Marry me, Rory."

A single tear tracked down Rory's face and her lips pressed together as she tried unsuccessfully to control the tears that followed.

He swept them from her cheeks with his thumbs and cradled her face in his hands. "Is this the woman who rarely cries?"

She shook her head. "No, this is the woman who'll be your wife."

He closed his eyes with relief and pressed his forehead to hers. Then he kissed her, grabbed her hand firmly within his and led the way back up the winding path to the castle.

There was only one way he could show her how he felt, and it wasn't through words.

EPILOGUE

Eighteen months later...

Rory emerged from the copse of chestnut trees where she'd been discussing the woodland with the estate manager, and looked around Senlisse with satisfaction. It was now the flourishing estate she'd once dreamed of. Thanks to Sahmir.

And that wasn't the only dream come true. She turned to watch Sahmir and their daughter, Ensiyette, emerge from the chateau. They were holding hands and Ensiyette was looking up at her Papa with an intense expression, chattering away in a language which only she knew, but which her doting Papa was prepared to pretend he understood.

Suddenly their two pure white saluki dogs came bounding towards Ensiyette and she ran off with them, looking likely to fall at any moment as she ran at full tilt on her chubby little legs down the slope to the wildflower meadow.

"Ensiyette!" Sahmir shouted, wincing as if he imagined her falling over. But she disappeared into the wildflower meadow, having somehow managed to remain upright. Sahmir's call brought forth Ensiyette's nanny who followed her down to the meadow.

Sahmir caught sight of Rory and walked over to her, shaking his head. "Our daughter is half-wild. I swear she talks that strange language of hers—half Arabic, half French —to the dogs and they understand."

Rory laughed and stretched up to kiss him. "I think you can be sure the dogs are only pretending they understand, like you."

"And how, dear wife, do you know this?"

"Because I was exactly the same. Maman used to say I talked more to my horses than to the family. Besides, what do you expect when we live half the time in each country, and she has a half-Arab half-French name?"

"'Little Ensiyeh'. I love that you suggested that name."

"Seemed fitting. We wouldn't be here if it weren't for your sister's wise words guiding you. I just hope Ensiyette has a fraction of your sister's wisdom." They both looked over to the meadow, where Ensiyette's dark curls could be seen, bobbing through the long grass, which was sprinkled with poppies and cornflowers, closely followed by the dogs and her nanny. Rory laughed. "Though I doubt it somehow. She's too much like me."

He shook his head, as he brushed some small twigs which had somehow attached themselves to Rory's old jersey. "Half-wild."

Rory slipped her arms around Sahmir and pulled him against her. "You wouldn't have me any other way, and you know it." She pressed her small pregnant bump against his stomach and smiled at his response.

"Um." He pushed the hair that had escaped from her ponytail back off her face. "If you've finished your work, maybe we've time for a little siesta?"

"I swear it was one of these siestas which was responsible for this." She patted her swelling stomach.

He brushed his lips against hers. "That's why I like living part of the time in Ma'in. Hot afternoons are for sleeping and—"

She robbed his words with a kiss that developed into more than just a kiss until they tore apart, breathless. "And so are cold afternoons." He tugged her hand and they walked quickly up to the chateau. "And lukewarm afternoons," she continued, as the walk turned into a run, "and everything in between."

∽

AFTERWORD

Thank you for reading *Claimed by the Sheikh*. I hope you enjoyed it! Reviews are always welcome—they help me, and they help prospective readers to decide if they'd enjoy the book.

The Desert Kings series comprises:

> Wanted: A Wife for the Sheikh
> The Sheikh's Bargain Bride
> The Sheikh's Lost Lover
> Awakened by the Sheikh
> Claimed by the Sheikh
> Wanted: A Baby by the Sheikh

The next book in the Desert Kings series features Daidan and Taina in *Wanted: A Baby by the Sheikh* (excerpt follows). Here's a review of *Wanted: A Baby by the Sheikh* to give you a taste of what to expect.

"...This story was Sooo WONDERFUL!! It had an understated

AFTERWORD

elegance, simple on the surface yet complex... I Loved it !!! I just Loved Taina and Daiden. I had my worries at 1st but I'm now In LOVE w/them and their world" (Amazon.com)

You can check out all my books on the following pages. And, if you'd like to know when my next book is available, you can sign up for my new release e-mail list via my website —www.dianafraser.com.

Happy reading!

Diana

WANTED: A BABY BY THE SHEIKH

BOOK 6 OF DESERT KINGS—DAIDAN AND TAINA

"You walked away from our wedding and kept on walking. And I hear nothing from you for a year, except a trail of credit card charges. Now you return saying you want our baby. What the hell is going on, Taina?" But Finnish heiress, Taina, can't answer Prince

Daidan's question without destroying his world. So Daidan comes up with a proposal of his own...

Excerpt

Prince Daidan ibn Saleh al-Fulan turned his back to the window. Behind him the glittering lights of Helsinki pierced the night sky like cut diamonds. "You still haven't told me why you've returned, what it is you want."

Taina Mustonen brushed her fingertips over the arctic white fur cushion, noticing with painful clarity how her fingers were so tense that their tips quivered. She sunk them deep into its pile so he wouldn't notice. "You're right. I do want something."

"What?"

She channelled the tension inside into a smile: tight at first but with focus it gentled into the mocking smile she desired. "I've decided to keep my side of the bargain."

He didn't speak at first but she could see the shock register in his eyes, even while he carefully schooled the rest of his expression into an uncommunicative mask. "To have our child?"

She took a long, deep breath. "Yes, I want our child."

His gaze narrowed. "You walked away from our wedding, just walked away and kept walking while I waited for you, not knowing. And I hear nothing from you except a trail of bank transactions, credit card bills, for over a year. Now, without explanation you return saying you want our baby. What the hell is going on, Taina?"

Buy Now!

ALSO BY DIANA FRASER

The Mackenzies
The Real Thing
The PA's Revenge
The Marriage Trap
The Cowboy's Craving
The Playboy's Redemption
The Lakehouse Café

New Zealand Brides
Yours to Give
Yours to Treasure
Yours to Cherish

Desert Kings
Wanted: A Wife for the Sheikh
The Sheikh's Bargain Bride
The Sheikh's Lost Lover
Awakened by the Sheikh
Claimed by the Sheikh
Wanted: A Baby by the Sheikh

Italian Romance
Perfect
Her Retreat
Trusting Him
An Accidental Christmas

Printed in Great Britain
by Amazon